# ATTACK OF THE METEOR MONSTERS

# Books by Chris Priestley

The Maudlin Towers series
*Curse of the Werewolf Boy*
*Treasure of the Golden Skull*
*Attack of the Meteor Monsters*

*

The Tales of Terror series
*Uncle Montague's Tales of Terror*
*Tales of Terror from the Black Ship*
*Tales of Terror from the Tunnel's Mouth*

*

*Mister Creecher*
*Through Dead Eyes*
*The Dead Men Stood Together*
*The Last of the Spirits*

# MAUDLIN TOWER

# ATTACK OF THE METEOR MONSTERS

Written and illustrated by
## CHRIS PRIESTLEY

BLOOMSBURY
CHILDREN'S BOOKS
LONDON OXFORD NEW YORK NEW DELHI SYDNEY

BLOOMSBURY CHILDREN'S BOOKS
Bloomsbury Publishing Plc
50 Bedford Square, London WC1B 3DP, UK

BLOOMSBURY, BLOOMSBURY CHILDREN'S BOOKS and the
Diana logo are trademarks of Bloomsbury Publishing Plc

First published in Great Britain in 2019 by Bloomsbury Publishing Plc

A catalogue record for this book is available from the British Library

ISBN: PB: 978-1-4088-7312-0; eBook: 978-1-4088-7313-7

2 4 6 8 10 9 7 5 3 1

Typeset by RefineCatch Limited, Bungay, Suffolk

Printed and bound in Great Britain by CPI Group (UK) Ltd, Croydon CR0 4YY

To find out more about our authors and books visit www.bloomsbury.com
and sign up for our newsletters

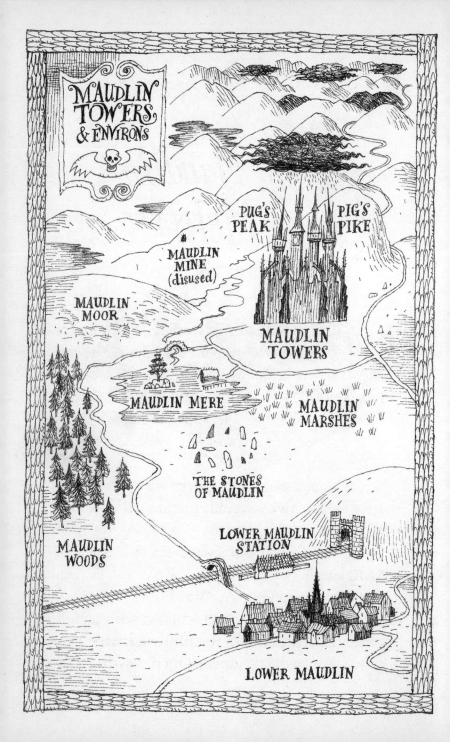

# 1 Maudlin Meteor

M ildew and Sponge were still gasping for breath at the top of Pig's Pike as the rest of the boys jogged their way back down. The sun was just beginning to rise and drizzle dribbled from the dark sky above them, polishing the blackened pinnacles of the grim and grimy Maudlin Towers.

'I had hoped our new sports master – *gasp* – might drop this twice-weekly torture, Mildew,' said Sponge with a sigh.

'I'm afraid all sports masters are evil, Sponge,' said Mildew.

'But why?' cried Sponge. 'Why?'

'No one knows why,' said Mildew with a sigh. 'They just are. It's one of those things that will never be fully explained. Like opera. Or chemistry.'

Sponge sighed again. Their new sports master, Mr Gruntforth, had proven to be every bit as horribly energetic and enthusiastic as Mr Stupendo and Mr Lithely before him. He was threatening to make the annual Fell-Running Tournament compulsory. They had thought all danger of having to compete in it had gone with the departure of Mr Stupendo.

'Do you ever wonder how Mr Stupendo got on when the time machine took him back to the age of the dinosaurs?' said Sponge.

'No,' said Mildew. 'Not really.'

'No,' said Sponge. 'Me neither.'

'We've had a lot of adventures lately,' said Mildew. 'What with the time machine, Vikings, werewolves, pirates and so forth. I'm hoping things might quieten down a bit. I'm growing rather nostalgic for the days when we were occasionally bored.'

'I know what you mean,' said Sponge. 'One can have too much excitement.'

Mildew nodded and then gazed off to the east, at the faint rays of the rising sun leaking out from under the blanket of cloud. He let out a groan.

'Look! It's barely light,' he said, wiping a coating of drizzle from his muzzle. 'I need my sleep, Sponge. I have a note from my mother to that effect.'

'So do I,' said Sponge with a frown.

'What?' said Mildew, seeing his friend's expression.

'What?' said Sponge, frown still very much in place.

'Is this about me supposedly snoring again?'

'Supposedly?' said Sponge. 'Ha!'

'How dare you "ha"!' said Mildew. 'I have never snored in my life. The very idea! The Mildews are known throughout Berkshire for their almost complete lack of snoring. It is another of your delusions, Sponge. I worry about you, I really –'

Suddenly there was a blinding flash of light and a terrifying roar as something large and fiery hurtled out of the clouds over their heads and slammed into the summit of Pug's Peak.

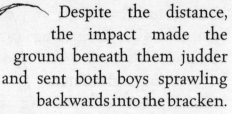

Despite the distance, the impact made the ground beneath them judder and sent both boys sprawling backwards into the bracken. When the friends got to their feet they stared in amazement, trying to come to terms with what their boyish eyes were seeing. There was a pale glow where the thing had crash-landed and an eerie, unearthly hum.

'Why are you making that eerie, unearthly hum, Sponge?' said Mildew.

'I always make an eerie, unearthly hum when I have the wibbles, Mildew.'

'Well, stop,' said Mildew. 'It's most distracting.'

'What *is* that, Mildew?' said Sponge with a whimper.

'I don't know, Sponge. Perhaps it's a meteor,' said Mildew.

'A meteor?' said Sponge.

'Yes,' said Mildew. 'There was a passing reference to them in The Bored Boy's Book of Moderately Diverting Things in the library.'

'I love that book.'

'Me too,' said Mildew.

'There aren't enough books of mildly interesting trivia.'

'I concur,' said Mildew. 'Perhaps it's time for us to fire off some more letters to the various publishing houses.'

'Ooh – yes,' said Sponge. 'They might even reply this time.'

'It's entirely possible. 'But –'

'Mildew!' cried Sponge. 'What's that?'

Peering across to Pug's Peak in the dawn half-light, the boys could just make out something stirring in the glow of the fallen object and then moving stealthily away down the hillside.

'Probably just sheep,' said Mildew. 'You know how sheep are.'

'I suppose …' said Sponge doubtfully. 'But they don't look like sheep to me.'

'Even sheep don't always look like sheep,' said Mildew. 'Not all the time. It depends what angle you look at them from.'

'You could say that about anything.'

'Exactly my point. Anyway – we should be getting back. The others must have seen and heard that monstrous impact and will be terribly worried about us.'

'You're right,' said Sponge.

The two boys set off down the side of Pig's Pike, casting only the occasional glance back in the direction of Pug's Peak and the crash site, which was almost silhouetted now against the gathering light of dawn.

## 2
## Plummeting Cheese

Mildew and Sponge returned to school, hurriedly changed out of their drizzle-soaked shorts and vests and into their school uniforms before scuttling along to the refectory for breakfast, eager to reassure the others they were safe. When they arrived, however, the rest of the boys gave every impression of not being in the least concerned about them.

'It's all right!' announced Mildew. 'Do not be alarmed. Worry not. We're completely fine. I trust we haven't spoiled your breakfast.'

The boys stared at them for a moment and then,

without response, returned to their previous conversations. Soon the room was filled again with chatter and clatter. Mildew and Sponge stared at each other for a moment before Mildew tried again.

'I said,' repeated Mildew, more loudly this time, 'worry not. Sponge and I are unharmed.'

'Why on earth would we worry about you?' said Kenningworth without even looking up.

'Did you not see it?' cried Mildew.

'See what?' said Kenningworth disinterestedly.

'The meteor!' said Mildew.

This did at least grab the attention of some of the boys, who turned to face him, although many of them wore expressions of doubt rather than interest.

'Did you say meteor?' said Furthermore.

'What nonsense is this?' said Kenningworth.

'It is not any kind of nonsense,' said Mildew, pushing out his chest. 'We could have been killed. Tell them, Sponge.'

'We could have been killed,' confirmed Sponge.

'And yet you appear to be utterly unscathed,' said

Kenningworth, flaring his nostrils. 'No trace of scathing at all. I've never seen two people less scathed. I wonder –'

'Oh, be quiet, Kenningworth,' said Mildew.

'What makes you think it was a meteor?' said Furthermore.

'Well, it fell out of the sky in a ball of fire,' Mildew replied. 'What else could it be?'

'Cheese?' said Hipflask.

'Cheese?' said Mildew. 'Are you suggesting a huge ball of flaming cheese slammed into the top of Pug's Peak?'

'My mother says cheese can make you see all kinds of things,' said Hipflask. 'Especially French cheese.'

Kenningworth chuckled.

'I'm with Hipflask's mother,' he said. 'You're seeing things.'

'It was not French cheese and we were not seeing things,' said Mildew firmly. 'It came hurtling out of the sky and crashed into Pug's Peak. There was a burning glow where it landed.'

'And there were things moving about,' said Sponge.

Here Sponge demonstrated the aforementioned moving about by a wiggling of his fingers.

'Things moving about?' said Kenningworth, peering at the wiggling fingers.

'Although they were probably just sheep,' said Mildew, frowning at Sponge. 'Ignore the sheep.'

'They didn't look like sheep to me,' said Sponge.

Kenningworth heaved a sigh, got up and looked out of the window towards Pug's Peak.

'Well, I can't see any sign of a glow,' he said, 'or anything else for that matter.'

The others joined him and, after a while, they turned with equal scepticism towards Mildew and Sponge.

'Well, the sun has come up a bit more than before,' said Mildew. 'You can't see the glow now.'

'Pah!' exclaimed Kenningworth.

To Mildew and Sponge's dismay, the boys returned to their seats and to their chatter as though nothing had occurred and as though Mildew and Sponge were not there at all.

'I wonder how long it would have taken them to notice had we never returned,' said Sponge forlornly.

'Never mind them,' said Mildew as they collected their bowls of lumpen porridge from Mrs Glump and sat down together at a different table.

'They don't believe us, Mildew,' said Sponge, gasping with the effort of forcing his spoon into the grey and grimly resistant porridge.

'We'll show them, Sponge,' said Mildew.

'How?'

'I don't know at the moment,' said Mildew. 'But we'll show them, mark my words. It might help matters if you didn't keep going on about sheep. It confuses things.'

'I'm not going on about sheep. I don't even think they were sheep. It's you who –'

'Do you see?' said Mildew. 'Even you're confused.'

# 3 A Kerfuffle in the Vestibule

With breakfast over, Mildew and Sponge and the other boys trooped unenthusiastically away to prepare for their first lessons. They had not gone far, however, when they noticed a kerfuffle in the vestibule.

'There's a kerfuffle in the vestibule,' said Mildew.

'What is the vestibule again?' said Sponge.

'A lobby area beside the main door to a building,' said Mildew.

'What?' said Sponge.

'The bit outside the Headmaster's office,' said Mildew. 'Really, Sponge, I wish you'd –'

They stopped to stare wide-eyed and wide-mouthed in horror. Sponge tried but failed to put his mounting dread into words, his chest beating as though it was host to an octopus playing the bongos.

Mildew had to give voice to Sponge's astonishment for him.

'Girls …'

It was true. Incredible though it seemed to all who observed it, this was indeed the case. None of the boys had ever in their entire lives seen so many girls gathered together at one time.

'How?' said Enderpenny, speaking for all of them. 'Why? What? When? Who?'

No answer was apparent to any of these important and searching questions. The world seemed simply to have gone mad. Perhaps it was the end of days. Chaos had been let loose and had the school in its wild and silly grip.

The Headmaster stood amid this herd of feminine incomers, talking to a tall and rather odd-looking woman who accompanied the girls. He turned suddenly to face the boys, making the more sensitive among them squeal.

'Ah,' he said with his usual crocodilian smile. 'Come here, come here.'

At this, the girls likewise turned towards them, chilling the blood of every boy present. Their twinkling eyes seemed to look into their very souls. Not one boy moved an inch.

'Come *here*,' said the Headmaster a little more firmly, and a little less smiley.

The boys edged forward like anxious piglets.

'We have some guests, as you can see,' said the Headmaster, waving his long fingers in indication. 'I trust you will show them every Maudlin courtesy while they are among us.'

The boys looked at the floor and mumbled something that could have been anything. The Headmaster waited for more and when it did not come he gave Mildew an encouraging nudge in the ear with his elbow.

'B-b-but … why, sir?' stammered Mildew in response.

'These delightful creatures have met with an unfortunate emergency while travelling this wild and windy country and have been forced to seek sanctuary at Maudlin Towers. Here is their Headmistress, Miss … ?'

'M … T … 2 … T.'

'Miss MT2T?'

'Affirmative,' she replied, her stilted outburst punctuated with the faintest of clanks and wheezes.

The boys took a nervous step backward.

'What an enchanting name,' said the Headmaster. 'Is it Welsh perhaps?'

'Wel … sh?' said Miss MT2T.

There was a pause. The Headmaster's grin wavered a little under the strain of anticipation. It became clear that this discussion of the origin of Miss MT2T's name had run its course.

'And you had an unfortunate incident with your carriage, I gather?' said the Headmaster eventually.

'Affirmative. One ... of our horse ... machines ... malfunctioned ...' said the Headmistress.

Mildew and Sponge exchanged a puzzled glance. Even allowing for the fact that she was a teacher, Miss MT2T was very, very odd indeed. The girls seemed to grow agitated as the boys stared at her.

'Yes, sir,' said one of them at the front. 'Exploded. Bang. Just like that.'

'Your horse exploded?' asked the Headmaster.

The girls nodded and after a moment or two Miss MT2T did likewise but with rather more squeaking.

'Horses are skittish creatures,' said the Headmaster with a nod. 'I've never entirely trusted them. I have similar reservations about geese.'

There was another long and awkward pause. Miss MT2T again seemed unwilling to add any more detail to the tale of their predicament. The Headmaster rocked back and forth on his shoes.

'But rest assured you will be made very welcome at Maudlin Towers,' he said at last. 'We do not have our own carriage, I'm afraid, but there is a train from Lower Maudlin every second Tuesday in the month. You shall be our guests until the next one leaves in five days' time.'

'You … are … very kind,' said Miss MT2T.

'Yes,' said one of the girls. 'Very kind, sir.'

'Poppynonsense,' said the Headmaster with a snort. 'This is England. We are renowned throughout the potato-eating world for our hospitality. You are part of the Maudlin family now. I shall have someone show you to your accommodation after you have had a chance to relax following your unpleasant mishap.'

The girls smiled and seemed relieved.

'Very well,' said the Headmaster after a few moments, clapping his hands together and making everyone jump. 'Miss MT2T and I will adjourn to my study. You boys can introduce yourselves to these young angels. Mingle, boys, mingle …'

The assembled group of boys and the corresponding group of girls stood looking at each other for several minutes before Mildew received a hefty shove in the back from Kenningworth and skidded into the void between them.

'Erm … good day,' said Mildew. 'My name is … My name is … My name is … What is my name again, Sponge?'

'Biscuit,' said Sponge helpfully.

'Try again, old button,' said Mildew.

'Mil … dew,' said Sponge.

'Yes, of course,' said Mildew. 'Well done. My name is Arthur Mildew. Of the Berkshire Mildews. You may have heard of us.'

Two of the girls turned to each other and shrugged.

'And this is my good friend, Algernon Spongely-Partwork,' he said. 'Although everyone calls him Sponge.'

'Or twerp,' said Kenningworth with a snigger.

'That's Kenningworth,' said Sponge. 'This is Enderpenny, Furthermore, Filbert, Hipflask …'

The boys each nodded at the mention of their name. The boys behind them stepped a couple of paces back, happy not to be included in Sponge's introductions.

'How do you do?' continued Sponge, a little breathlessly now, sweat beginning to trickle down his face.

'How do we do what?' said one of the girls.

'I … that is … well …' gibbered Sponge.

Mildew placed a consoling hand on his friend's shoulder and tried again.

'What are *your* names, might we enquire?' asked Mildew.

'My name?' said the first girl. 'Er … my name is …'

Mrs Glump went past with a trolley full of breakfast things.

'Milk,' she said.

'Milk?' said Mildew. 'As in … well, milk?'

'Yes, Milk,' she said.

'What a … what a … erm … name,' said Mildew.

'And yours?' said Sponge, looking at her friend.

'Who, me?' the friend replied.

She gazed around in what looked like panic. The door to the trophy room was open.

'Spoon,' she said. 'My name is Spoon.'

'Spoon?' said Sponge.

'That's right.'

'Oh,' said Sponge. 'Lovely.'

No one quite knew what to say next, and there followed a great deal of shoelace inspection and fingernail fiddling before Mildew summoned up the courage to go on.

'Have you come far?' he asked.

'Quite far, yes,' said Milk.

Spoon and Sponge stared at each other. There were no questions left to ask and yet the girls still gazed at them expectantly. What more could they reasonably want?

'What is this?' said Milk, looking at the broken and repaired bust outside the Headmaster's office. 'It looks rather like …'

She pointed at Sponge.

'Yes,' said Mildew with a forced chuckle. 'We've often laughed about that, haven't we, Sponge?'

Mildew and Sponge cast a furtive glance at each other. It looked like Sponge because it was Sponge, but how could they ever explain the existence of a Roman bust of a Maudlin schoolboy? Kenningworth leaned forward, peering at it.

'It does bear a startling resemblance to you, now she comes to mention it. How have I not noticed that before?'

Sponge wanted to say, 'Because you're a self-obsessed blot,' but he thought it best not to. There were so many things that Sponge wanted to say but didn't. In fact the things he didn't say outnumbered the things he did. By quite some way.

'Why is it broken?' said Spoon.

'Ah,' said Mildew. 'That's rather a long story and –'

Big Brian, the school bell, clanged its mighty

brain-rattling clang, shaking Maudlin Towers to its very foundations as usual, and Mildew and Sponge had never been so relieved to hear its din.

In fact, all the boys seemed relieved and were unusually eager to head for their lessons. For Mildew and Sponge this meant the most dreadful of all starts to the day – double maths with Mr Painly.

They left the girls with a swift farewell and wandered into Mr Painly's classroom, slumping themselves down as their maths teacher added some more digits to a baffling equation on the blackboard.

'I trust you didn't find the homework too difficult,' said Mr Painly.

There was a collective groan from the boys so pitiful it would have tugged a tear from the eye of even the most heartless and uncaring of dentists.

'I'm not sure I can cope,' whispered Sponge, 'with having g ...'

'With having what, old kipper?' whispered Mildew.

'With having g ...' repeated Sponge.

'Spit it out, Sponge!' hissed Mildew.

Sponge lifted a trembling finger and pointed instead. Mildew gasped. Some of the girls had followed them in. Mr Painly dropped his papers in surprise when he turned to see them. The girl called Milk raised her hand as alarm began to spread through the room.

'Sir,' she said. 'We have been told to join in with the class while we are at the school. If that's all right with you, sir. The Headmaster insisted.'

'Of course, of course,' said Mr Painly with a smile. 'The more the merrier.'

He dropped some more papers, picked them up, coughed, adjusted his moustache two or three times and continued.

'I have to warn you that we are flying at a rather high altitude, mathematics-wise. Please don't feel embarrassed to ask for help if you can't keep up.'

Mildew and Sponge noticed the girls glance at each other.

'Sir,' said Milk with a smile. 'We have long since overtaken anything your human mathematics can conceive of.'

'Human mathematics?' said Mr Painly. 'A curious way to put it.'

Mildew noticed Spoon nudge Milk hard in the ribs and whisper to her. She said nothing more.

'Very well,' Mr Painly continued with a frown and a sniff. 'Let's see whether our "human mathematics", as you put it, can still throw up the odd surprise for you …'

When Big Brian rang its cacophonous chimes for the end of the lesson, Mildew and Sponge saw the girls trudge out with the weary, stunned and confused expressions they recognised all too well.

'Not to worry,' said Mildew to Milk. 'He has that effect on everyone.'

'But … but … but …' said Milk.

'We know,' said Mildew consolingly. 'Maths is an unpleasant business.'

'It made no sense,' said Spoon, staring off into the distance. 'No sense at all.'

Sponge nodded.

'That's maths for you,' he said. 'It's simply not meant to be understood.'

# 5 A Long Gothic Novel full of Pitiless Gloom

The boys trudged off to their next lesson in a state of fevered agitation. Girls *and* maths! It was far too much for them to deal with. Sponge actually felt like his brain might go pop at any moment.

'I feel like my brain might go pop,' said Sponge, 'at any moment.'

'Courage, my friend,' said Mildew. 'It's double English now. Your brain can have a rest.'

But the imminent brain-popping sensation was not entirely relieved when Mildew and Sponge discovered that the girls intended to attend all their classes and found them already seated in the English classroom.

Their English teacher, Miss Bronteen, had not been the same since her beloved had come back with the pirate crew that had taken over Maudlin Towers some weeks earlier. Miss Bronteen had not been the same before then, to be fair, but she was now even less so.

Whereas once she had stared out at the breeze-befuddled moors she used to roam as a youngling, Miss Bronteen now stared at planks of wood. She had enlisted the services of Mr Scurry, the caretaker, to have the window boarded up, and so, though she stood in precisely the same place as ever she did, Miss Bronteen now gazed upon the roughly hewn wooden screen Mr Scurry had erected to block the view.

'Take out your copies of *Blithering Abbey*, turn to page 397 and –'

'Miss?' said one of the girls who had joined the class.

There was a collective gasp from the boys at the very notion of interrupting Miss Bronteen. She turned round slowly.

'So it is true,' she said with the arch of an eyebrow. 'There are indeed young ladies here at the school. Who would ever have thought it possible? What is it, my dear?'

'What should we do, miss?' said Spoon. 'We don't have copies of Blithering Abbey, nor have we read it.'

Miss Bronteen stared wide-eyed and trembled from temple to toe.

'Have not read it?' she cried, her voice quivering with disbelief. 'Have not read it? What is the world coming to? Every girl should read Blithering Abbey.'

'Sorry, miss.'

Miss Bronteen sighed.

'I suppose we must make allowances for our visitors, boys. So rather than read Blithering Abbey, we shall instead create our own work of literature.'

This news was greeted with a rich variety of whines and muttering which Miss Bronteen chose to ignore. Taking a deep breath she turned away from her pupils.

'I want you to begin work on a very, very long Gothic novel,' she said, speaking into the planks. 'A novel full of pitiless gloom and dankness, and dank, pitiless gloominess. I want bleakness. I want despair. And I want it by Wednesday. Begin.'

When the class had ended, Mildew and Sponge waited behind until the rest of the boys and their female visitors had trooped off to break.

'Miss?' said Mildew.

'Yes?' said Miss Bronteen. 'Wherefore do you linger, boys?'

'Sorry, miss?' said Sponge.

'Why are you still here?' she said with a sigh.

'You were a girl once, miss,' said Mildew. 'In a way.'

'That is correct,' she said. 'Although it seems a very long time ago now.'

'A very, very long time ago,' said Sponge.

Miss Bronteen frowned.

'Only Sponge and I were wondering if you might have any advice on how to communicate with the feminine types we now have among us. The Headmaster has asked us to ensure their well-being during their stay. But we are not used to talking to the other gender, miss.'

Miss Bronteen smiled and Mildew took out a notebook and pencil and waited for her words of wisdom.

'Do not be afraid of them, boys,' said Miss Bronteen. 'They are human, just like you, after all.'

'I suppose …' said Mildew.

'All I would say …' said Miss Bronteen.

'Yes, miss?' asked Sponge expectantly.

'All I would ask,' she continued, 'is that you do not lead them on a foolish dance across the moors for months on end, only to savagely and cruelly crush their dreams and expectations and leave their hearts bruised and battered and grievously wounded, casting them aside like an old bonnet …'

'Well, I shouldn't think we'll –'

'And then return years later to rekindle those

dormant dreams and dangle a glimpse of happiness only to snatch it away at the last minute and snuff out the candle of hope forever. Would you promise me that, boys? Would you?'

'Yes, miss,' said Mildew and Sponge.

'Good boys,' she said, and turned back to the blocked-up window. 'Leave me now. I would be alone.'

Mildew consulted his notes as the two boys stood together in the cloisters.

'Not an awful lot in the way of practical help, Sponge,' he said.

'No,' said Sponge.

'I wonder if we might be better served by a visit to the library.'

'For books about girls, you mean?' said Sponge.

'Girls?' said Mildew. 'No – I think we have to accept that girls will forever remain a mystery to us, Sponge. No – I was meaning something that will help us in convincing the others about our meteor.'

Mildew and Sponge were heading down the corridor on the way to the library when they turned a corner and, to their immense agitation, bumped into the two girls they had spoken to earlier – Milk and Spoon.

'Hello,' said Milk.

'Ah … yes … indeed … quite,' said Mildew, looking at his watch and realising too late that he didn't have one.

'Where are you going?' asked Spoon.

'Going?' squeaked Sponge with a slight splutter. 'Nowhere.'

'You have to be going somewhere,' said Milk.

'Oh, Sponge and I often go nowhere,' said Mildew. 'We're famous for it. We went nowhere twice yesterday, didn't we, Sponge? Three times if you count geography with Mr Drumlin.'

Sponge stared at Spoon but said not a word.

'Sponge!' repeated Mildew.

'Biscuit,' said Sponge dreamily.

'Biscuit?' said Milk.

'Don't mind Sponge,' said Mildew. 'He often says biscuit when he can't think of what else to say. Biscuits aren't very far from his thoughts, you see. His head is basically a kind of prickly biscuit barrel.'

'What is so fascinating about biscuits?' said Spoon.

Both boys rocked sideways with shock.

'What is so fascinating about biscuits?' they gasped. 'What can you mean? They are the food of the gods!'

'We've never actually tasted them,' said Milk.

'Never … tasted … them … ?' said Sponge. 'But …'

Both girls shook their heads. Sponge reached into his pocket and pulled out a paper bag.

'I usually have some on me in case of emergencies,' said Sponge, offering the bag to the girls.

They eyed it warily and then Milk reached

in and gingerly took a biscuit. It was a ginger biscuit. Spoon did the same and bit into hers. Both girls nibbled with increasing confidence and their eyes opened wide.

'Delicious,' said Milk. 'I don't think I've tasted anything better this side of the Zygor Cluster.'

'Shhh!' said Spoon.

'The Zygor Cluster?' said Mildew.

'Yes,' said Milk. 'It's near … Birmingham.'

Neither Mildew nor Sponge could think of any response to this and so with a parting smile and nod, they scuttled off to the library and found Miss Foxing, the school librarian, sitting at her desk.

'Good morning, miss,' said Sponge.

'Good morning, boys,' she said. 'What are we after today? I'm afraid I'm still waiting for the new Finlay Feathering mystery, Mildew – and *Every Boy's Book of Biscuits* is still out, Sponge.'

'Rather amusingly,' said Mildew with a chuckle, 'Sponge here imagined we were coming to the library to look for books about girls …'

Miss Foxing raised an eyebrow.

'Girls, you say?' she said, sitting back in her chair.

'But we are actually looking for –'

'Could this have anything to do with

our young visitors?' said Miss Foxing.

'But –' began Mildew.

'Yes,' said Sponge. 'The Headmaster has charged us with mingling with the said girls but they are a fathomless mystery, miss.'

Miss Foxing came round from behind her desk and, indicating they should follow, took them to an area of the library they had never noticed before – despite it being only a couple of feet from the entrance.

'Perhaps you mean books like these …' said Miss Foxing.

'Good Lord,' said Mildew, taking one of the books from the shelf. 'This is exactly the sort of thing. Look, Sponge. *Every Girl's Book of Fabulous Females*. It even has a girl on the cover.'

'So does this one,' said Sponge, looking on in awe. 'The Adventurous Girl's Guide to High Jinx.'

'They all have girls on the cover,' said Mildew, taking down others at random.

The books were all in pristine condition.

'They seem brand new,' said Mildew. 'When did you get them, miss? Why have we never noticed them before?'

'Some have been here for many years, Mildew,' said Miss Foxing. 'It's just that you boys have never shown the slightest bit of interest in them.'

'Extraordinary,' said Mildew.

Mildew and Sponge sat at a table and began to pull titles off the shelves at random, non-fiction at first, but after a while they began to leaf through novels.

'Sponge,' said Mildew after a while, looking up and over the cover of Molly Musket Strikes Again.

'Yes?' said Sponge, clearly engrossed in reading Samantha Swanly Saves the Day.

'I think we have allowed ourselves to be distracted from our mission.'

'Oh – I think you're right, Mildew!'

The boys returned to Miss Foxing.

'Can I be of assistance?' said Miss Foxing with a smile. 'Again?'

'Yes, miss,' said Sponge. 'We need your help.'

'What can I do for you now, boys?' she said.

'We are looking for books about meteors and all that kind of caper. Do you have anything like that?'

'I think there might be the very book for you in the section you've just been in, actually,' said Miss Foxing.

'Really?' said Mildew.

'Yes,' said Miss Foxing, wandering over and taking a large book from the bottom shelf. 'Here we are.'

'*Everything Any Girl Could Reasonably Want to Know about the Universe,*' said Mildew, reading the title on the cover.

'That seems perfect,' said Sponge. 'Thank you, miss.'

Mildew opened the book and the boys began flicking through the pages expectantly. About thirty pages in, the pages became blank and continued blank until the end.

'There seems to be something wrong with the book, Sponge,' said Mildew.

'Yes,' said Sponge. 'It's almost entirely empty. Look, there's a note here on the last page. It says: "The publishers apologise for the lack of information hereafter. The universe is very large but our knowledge of it is very small. Perhaps one day these pages will be filled as new discoveries come to light. Until then, sorry ..."'

The boys sighed and slumped over the desk.

'Wait a minute, Sponge,' said Mildew. 'Look at this – on the last page with anything useful on it.'

Sponge followed Mildew's finger to a drawing of a cluster of stars.

'The Zygor Cluster,' said Mildew.

'I had no idea Birmingham was so far away,' said Sponge.

'No,' said Mildew. 'It's not. The Zygor Cluster is in outer space.'

'Then why would Milk and Sponge say it was near Birmingham?' asked Sponge.

'Why indeed?' said Mildew, stroking his chin.

'Look at this, Mildew,' said Sponge, pointing to another page.

An illustration showed a strange object hurtling past planets and stars. It had tiny windows through which the silhouetted occupants could be glimpsed. Underneath it were the words: *Artist's impression of a space-carriage.*

The two boys gasped and stared at each other, wide-eyed.

'A space-carriage!' they cried.

'Shhhh,' said Miss Foxing.

# Mildew and Sponge Investigate

The boys left the library, edging round each corner with great trepidation, making sure that there were no random girls loitering about ready to pounce. They sat down on their favourite step in the cloisters to mull things over.

'It's awfully annoying that the other boys don't believe us about the meteor,' said Sponge.

'Pah!' said Mildew. 'It's all Kenningworth's fault, the trotter. If only we could prove what we saw.'

'But how would we do that?' said Sponge.

Mildew got up, placed a fist on each hip and stared off, slightly upwards and to one side.

'What are you doing?' said Sponge.

'I'm adopting a heroic pose,' said Mildew. 'Statues do it all the time.'

'Oh,' said Sponge. 'Why, might I ask? You look like

you are about to make an announcement of some kind.'

'I am! We shall scale Pug's Peak and find the meteor!'

'Did you say, "scale Pug's Peak"?' said Sponge tremulously.

Mildew strode towards his friend and clasped a hand on each of his shoulders, staring into his eyes with what he hoped was a look of fierce determination.

'I did,' said Mildew. 'And what's more, we shall do it this very instant!'

'What about art with Mr Riddell? We are supposed to be doing another drawing of the torments of the damned in hell.'

'Oh, he'll never notice once the room is filled with charcoal dust,' said Mildew. 'Come on!'

Mildew set off but his friend remained rooted to his step.

'But scaling Pug's Peak …' said Sponge, his bottom lip wibbling.

'Don't you see, old friend?' said Mildew. 'Kenningworth will think we've made it up unless we bring back evidence.'

'But I still don't see how we will do that, Mildew,' said Sponge.

'I was just coming to that, old sprout,' said Mildew triumphantly. 'We shall take a piece of paper and a pencil and I shall draw it. Let them try and argue with that!'

'You are a genius, Mildew,' said Sponge.

Mildew did not see the need to argue.

The two friends headed out of the school and along the bracken-bordered track that led to the base of Pug's Peak. Taking a deep breath, they began the ascent.

The drizzle had stopped but the bracken and the many spider webs that laced their way among the fronds were beaded with water droplets which twinkled as they caught the light from the milky morning sun.

'Who would … *gasp* … ever have … *gasp* … thought … we would ever … climb a … *gasp* … hill … by choice?' gasped Sponge as they finally neared the summit.

'In … *gasp* … deed,' said Mildew, taking a deep breath. 'These are strange times, old … *gasp* … sausage.'

'Look … *gasp*,' said Sponge. 'There!'

Sure enough, the boys could see something smooth embedded in the peaty earth. It was splashed with mud, and clumps of earth and stones had been thrown this way and that with the impact. Mildew and Sponge could feel the warmth still radiating from it.

'I thought a meteor would be more … meteory,' said Sponge as they peered at the curiously smooth, metallic-looking thing.

'Me too,' said Mildew.

The boys edged closer to the mysterious object and noticed that the visible part of it was only the tip of something much larger that was embedded in the ground.

'Look, Sponge,' said Mildew. 'Can you see?'

There was the outline of a hatch in the whatever-it-was, with strange markings next to it.

Mildew reached out a shaking hand and rapped on the whatever-it-was with his knuckles. There was a hollow-sounding clang.

'A hollow-sounding clang,' observed Sponge. 'That's an odd sound for a rock to make.'

'I think we may need to reassess our assessment that this is a rock, Sponge,' said Mildew. 'Rocks rarely clang in my experience. I think that whatever the whatever-this-is is, it seems to be some sort of vehicle.'

'A vehicle?' said Sponge. 'What sort of a vehicle?'

'A vehicle from the stars! A space-carriage!'

Sponge gazed in wonder for a moment before leaning forward and rapping on the space-carriage with his knuckles.

'Hello?' he called. 'Hello? Is there anyone there?'

Mildew hurled himself towards his friend with uncharacteristic urgency, pulling him away.

'Sponge!' he hissed. 'What on earth are you doing?'

'I'm trying to introduce myself,' said Sponge. 'It's only polite.'

'Only polite?' hissed Mildew. 'We aren't visiting your Aunt Bernard, Sponge. Who knows what kind of monsters might be inside.'

'Monsters?' said Sponge, taking several steps back.

'Yes, monsters,' said Mildew. 'With teeth and boggly eyes and so forth.'

Sponge whimpered.

'Luckily it seems as though the carriage is deserted. But we can't be too careful. Finlay Feathering had a similar encounter recently in *Lady Viola and the Vipers from Venus*,' said Mildew.

'You don't think they are snakes, do you, Mildew?' said Sponge. 'I don't like snakes.'

'They could be anything,' said Mildew. 'Anything at all.'

Sponge gasped and remembered his earlier glimpse of mysterious movements on the fellside.

'You don't think –'

'Of course! I told you they weren't sheep, Sponge,' said Mildew.

'No, you didn't,' said Sponge. 'You told me they were!'

'Let's not bicker about the details,' said Mildew. 'The main thing is we seem to be dealing with a carriage of unknown origin and creatures from another world!'

Sponge whimpered.

'I'm having a fit of the wibbles, Mildew.'

'I'm feeling a touch wibblish myself, old mousse.'

'What should we do, Mildew?'

'I'm for steadfastly heading back to school before whoever-it-is or whatever-they-are come back,' said Mildew.

'Agreed,' said Sponge.

'But first ...' said Mildew.

He took out his paper and pencil and began to draw. After a couple of minutes he showed Sponge the smudged and spidery drawing.

'Let them argue with that!' declared Sponge.

# 8 Unidentified Falling Object

The boys were insensible with exhaustion by the time they returned to the school, staggering and stumbling into the cloisters. Only their desire to inform the other boys kept them upright.

'What's the matter with you two?' said

Furthermore. 'You look like you've been up Pug's Peak and back.'

The rest of the boys erupted into laughter at the preposterousness of this thought.

'We ... *gasp* ... have, actually,' said Sponge,

holding on to the door frame for support.

There was even more enthusiastic laughter. Mildew stepped forward and took a deep breath.

'Modify your mirth,' he said, swaying slightly. 'My bristly-pated associate tells the truth.'

'Pah!' said Kenningworth. 'Why on earth would you two lumps of trifle choose to engage in any exercise voluntarily?'

'Because,' said Mildew, 'we were investigating the UFO!'

'The UFO?' said Furthermore.

'The Unidentified Falling Object,' said Mildew. 'The one we mentioned earlier.'

Furthermore nodded.

'Not this nonsense with the so-called meteor again?' said Kenningworth with a groan.

'That's just it,' said Mildew. 'We don't think it is a meteor now.'

'Ha!' said Kenningworth. 'I knew you'd change your tune.'

'We are not changing our tune!' said Sponge.

'We are a bit,' said Mildew.

'Oh – yes, I suppose we are.'

'So if it isn't a meteor, what is it?' said Furthermore.

'We believe it is some kind of carriage.'

'A carriage?' said Kenningworth. 'What sort of

carriage would fall from the sky, you chump?'

'A carriage from the stars!' cried Sponge. 'A space-carriage!'

'What? There's no such thing,' said Kenning-worth.

'And yet there it is!' cried Mildew, wide-eyed, pointing in the direction of Pug's Peak. 'And not only that, the things Sponge thought were sheep were quite possibly the alien occupants!'

'You said they were sheep!' said Sponge.

'Never mind that now,' said Mildew.

'What?' said Kenningworth.

'We have been invaded by creatures from another world!' cried Mildew.

His dramatic outburst was greeted by baffled silence from the listening boys. They looked over to the other side of the cloisters, where most of the girls were sitting together.

'What are you blathering about?' said Kenning-worth eventually. 'They are a party of schoolgirls.'

'Not them, you turbot,' said Mildew. 'Actual aliens. From a different planet. From Mars or Venus or some-such heavenly body. We saw them.'

'What rot,' said Kenningworth, turning to the others. 'This is typical gibberish from them. Do you remember when they thought the school had been taken over by pirates?'

'Arrr. It *was* taken over by pirates,' said Enderpenny.

'Aye,' said Hipflask.

'Yes, well ...' said Kenningworth, waving away this objection. 'But what proof do you have for this poppycock?'

Mildew reached into his pocket and took out his drawing, laying it on the table and flattening it out.

'There!' he cried.

'Oh my stars,' said Furthermore in astonishment. 'It's true!'

'Do you still have that telescope of yours, Sponge?' said Enderpenny.

'Yes,' said Sponge.

'Come on then!' said Enderpenny.

The boys all set off to the dorm to get Sponge's telescope. They had not gone very far before they once again came face to face with Milk and Spoon.

'Hello again,' said Spoon.

'Hello,' said Sponge.

'Where are you going now?' asked Milk.

'Oh, we're just –'

'Ah,' said the Headmaster, looming

up behind them with his usual supernatural stealth. 'How are you getting along with our guests?'

'Famously, sir,' said Mildew.

The other boys murmured in agreement.

'Yes,' said Spoon. 'They are being most attentive.'

'Excellent,' said the Headmaster, who they now noticed had a small boy from the lower years in his charge.

'But we don't want to keep you, sir,' said Enderpenny. 'You look like you might be in a hurry.'

'Oh – yes,' he said. 'Just delivering young Slipshod here to the healing arms of Nurse Leecham.'

At the sound of her name the school nurse opened the door to her office and peered at poor Slipshod.

''E needs bleedin' again, sir,' said Mrs Leecham.

'But I've only twisted my ankle,' said the mite as he was pulled inside the office and the bolts were rammed home. The Headmaster bowed his farewell and went away down the corridor, humming to himself.

'My advice is, try not to have any need of medical attention during your stay in Maudlin Towers,' said Mildew to Milk and Spoon. 'But I'm afraid now we must dash as we are on a bit of a mission.'

The boys scampered to the dorm, grabbed the telescope from Sponge's locker and then stealthily

took the stairs to the roof.
They edged along the
parapet and among the
many pinnacles, pedi-
ments and chimneys until
they crowded together
at the battlemented wall
that gave them a clear
view towards Pug's Peak.
Mildew took the telescope
and peered into it.

'I can just make it out,' he said, handing the
telescope to Enderpenny. 'Look – just to the right
of the highest rock.'

'He's right,' said Enderpenny. 'See, Kenningworth?'

After a cursory look through the telescope,
Kenningworth was forced to admit that there did
seem to be something there.

'But it could be anything,' he was quick to add.

'There's nothing for it,' said Enderpenny. 'We
need to go and take a look for ourselves.'

'Imagine,' said Furthermore, 'if we should be the
first humans ever to encounter alien life forms.
That really would be something. Imagine what
wonders we might discover. Think of what we
might learn.'

'Yes,' said Kenningworth with sudden enthusiasm for the venture. 'Imagine what the newspapers would pay for a story like that. I'm with Enderpenny and Furthermore. We need to go up there and see what's what.'

'Excellent idea,' said Mildew, nodding sagely. 'Sponge and I will have a reviving biscuit or three in the dorm and await your return with interest.'

'You have to come as well,' said Footstool. 'You need to show us where it is.'

'But –' said Sponge with a hint of whimper.

'Come on!' said Kenningworth.

Mildew and Sponge hung their heads and followed the boys out of the school.

# Another UFO

Mildew and Sponge collapsed in twitching exhaustion as the boys reached the top of Pug's Peak once again and all they could do was feebly point in the general direction of the mysterious object. It was several minutes before they had the energy to join their fellows in contemplation of it.

'It could still be anything,' said Kenningworth, staring at the mysterious object embedded in the peat.

'Like what?' said Furthermore, leaning forward.

'I don't know,' said Kenningworth, flaring his nostrils. 'I'm not an expert.'

Furthermore edged even closer.

'These markings are interesting,' he said.

'Yes,' said Mildew. 'Sponge and I noticed those.

57

What do you think they are?'

'I rather think they may be letters or numbers,' he said. 'In a strange language.'

'French?' suggested Enderpenny.

'Stranger still,' said Furthermore.

'Stranger than French?' gasped Enderpenny in utter disbelief. 'What wizardry is this?'

'Look,' said Furthermore, indicating a large flat button with a prod of his finger. 'I wonder what this does.'

A door hissed open and the boys all took a step back and gasped, half expecting something to rush out. It was a few tense moments before they plucked up enough courage to push Mildew and Sponge towards the opening.

'Go and see what's in there, Sponge,' said Kenningworth, giving him a helpful shove.

'What?' said Sponge, staggering forward. 'Why me?'

'Well said,' said Mildew, pushing forward, giving Sponge a nudge of his own and sending his friend tumbling into the alien carriage. After a moment's silence there came a small voice.

'I'm all right,' said Sponge feebly, his faint voice echoing.

'What can you see?' shouted Kenningworth.

'Not a lot,' said Sponge. 'It's very dark.'

'Probably best not to touch anything,' said Furthermore.

'Oh,' said Sponge. 'I wish you'd –'

Sponge was suddenly jettisoned from the carriage, landing head first in the bracken behind them. The door hissed shut behind him.

'I touched something,' explained Sponge, getting to his feet. 'Sorry.'

After much prodding, the boys had to accept the door was not going to open again. Kenningworth even kicked it a few times in frustration but succeeded only in hurting his toe.

'Bizarre though it may be,' said Furthermore, 'it looks as though Mildew and Sponge are right in every regard. This does indeed appear to be some sort of craft or vessel from another world. And it does seem to have crash-landed on our planet.'

'Nonsense,' said Kenningworth. 'It's probably some old steam engine from Maudlin Mine.'

'That can fly?' asked Mildew. 'And then somehow crashed back to earth?'

'We only have your word for it that it crashed at all,' said Kenningworth. 'And your word is about as useful as a –'

Suddenly there was a great roaring noise that grew in volume until it was deafeningly loud and the boys looked up in horror to see a huge ball of fire rushing towards them out of the sky.

They threw themselves to the ground, each imagining it was their last moment alive, when, right at the last second, the plummeting object whooshed over them and landed a hundred yards away, making the earth shake and tremble. It was several seconds before they could hear anything but the roar of its passing.

'What was that?' said Sponge, shaking and trembling.

'I think it was another of whatever this is,' said Mildew, getting to his feet and pointing to the original mysterious object.

'That's rather a coincidence, don't you think?' said Furthermore as he was helped up by Hipflask.

The boys gathered together to look at the crash site of this new arrival.

'Maybe it's an invasion,' said Enderpenny.

'You think there will be more?' asked Sponge, looking up at the clouds. 'Because if you do I'm for heading back to Maudlin Towers.'

'I think the pimple may have a point,' said Kenningworth. 'Why don't we –'

But just at that moment a dazzling beam of light burst forth from the newly arrived craft and hit the boys. They froze – partly from fear but mostly because the beam of light itself seemed to have some sort of control over them.

'*Wigwagwigwagwigwagwigwag?*' said a booming voice.

# 10 Giant Mechanical Spiders

There was something about the tone of the booming, mysterious voice that suggested a question but the boys had absolutely no idea what it was saying.

'Wigwagwigwagwigwagwigwag?' it repeated, but louder and more insistently.

The boys whimpered.

There followed what they assumed was a conversation between the owner of that booming voice and the owner of another booming voice, each equally unintelligible. After a while the boys heard something like a sigh and a clanking and wheezing noise.

After a few seconds the wheezing and clanking grew in volume and two massive mechanical spiders loomed menacingly into view.

The voice appeared to be coming from a glowing orb atop each of the spiders.

'Aaaaaaargh!' squealed the boys as the beam of light loosened its grip.

'*Wigwagwigwagwigwagwigwag?*' boomed the voice again.

'We don't understand!' yelled Mildew. 'Who are you? What do you want from us? And will it be painful?'

Another muttered alien conversation took place and then, out of the glare of the beam, two cables came snaking towards the boys and towards Mildew and Sponge in particular.

There was a suction cup at the end of each cable and they landed with a plop on to the quivering heads of Mildew and Sponge. After a few seconds, the suction cups plopped off again and the cables retracted as the two boys collapsed to the ground.

'Good,' said the booming voice as Mildew and Sponge got to their feet. 'Now we have absorbed your Earthly language. This will aid communication.'

'Yes,' said the other. 'Although I think we should just vaporise the whole planet and be done with it.'

'Oh, you always want to vaporise everything,' said the first.

'I do not.'

'You do and you know you do.'

The other didn't reply straight away.

'It is a strange tongue …' it said presently. 'And also, in other news, I feel a little odd.'

'Agreed,' said the first. 'I do not feel quite myself either.'

They seemed to have forgotten the boys entirely, but then they suddenly released them from the grip of the beam and the boys fell into a gibbering mass, immediately turning to run away.

'Stay where you are!' boomed one of the aliens. 'No one runs from the Neenor!'

'Everyone runs from the Neenor,' said the other.

'Oh,' said the first with a horrible chuckle. 'Come to think of it, I suppose you're right. Why is that?'

'I have no idea,' said the other. 'I think we look rather splendid, old comet.'

'Agreed,' said the first. 'Stay where you are!'

The trembling boys stopped in their tracks and slowly turned round to see the mechanical spiders clanking and wheezing as their enormous black legs brought them looming closer. Huge mechanical gnashers gnashed above them.

'We are the Neenor,' said the nearest spider. 'We are here as representatives of the Mordentor Federation. Obey and you will be spared. I am Zigg and this is my associate, Tarduz. We are from the planet Marzz.'

'Mars?' said Mildew. 'I told you they might be from Mars, Sponge.'

'No, not Mars,' said Zigg. 'Marzz. A different place altogether. Mars is soooo boring. Have you been there?'

'No,' said Mildew. 'Not really.'

'Well, take our word for it,' said Tarduz with a snort of derision. 'If you like dust, it's great. Do you like dust?'

'Not especially,' said Sponge.

'Well, then,' said Zigg.

'W-w-what do you want from us?' asked Mildew.

'We will ask the questions!' boomed Zigg.

The boys cowered in fear. A silence of several minutes ensued.

'Well?' said Mildew.

'Oh. Yes. Lost my thread – sorry. We are looking for criminal aliens from one of our outposts on Teasel 12, charged with criminal acts against the Federation. As loyal subjects of the Federation you are compelled to hand them over or face the consequences as stipulated in Article 7198d of the Mordentor Federation Code.'

'The Mordentor Federation?' said Mildew. 'I've never heard of it. Have you, Sponge?'

'No,' said Sponge. 'How about you, Furtherm–'

'Never heard of it?' yelled Zigg. 'Never heard of it? You were annexed into the Mordentor Federation sixty-five million of your Earth years ago.'

'But there were no humans on Earth back then,' said Furthermore. 'That was the age of the dinosaurs. It's a common misconception that man and dinosaur existed at the same t–'

'Silence!' yelled Zigg. 'You are mistaken. There was an Earthloid there at that time. He was seated in a great throne. His head was as smooth as the moons of Wiffwaff. His facial hair was as luscious as the tails of the heffloids of the Forest Sector on Vibblon 7.'

'Oh no …' said Mildew.

'What?' said Kenningworth.

'Mr Stupendo!' said Mildew and Sponge together.

'What?' said Furthermore. 'Mr Stupendo our old sports teacher?'

'I fear so,' said Mildew.

'Yes,' said Zigg. 'You see. You've heard of him. But we never use his Earth name. It lacks respect. You must call him the Great One.'

'The Great One?' said Mildew. 'Are you sure?'

'The Great One. He signed the relevant paperwork on your behalf before he left,' said Tarduz. 'It was all quite legal and above board. One of the large lizard creatures you call dinosaurs ate his throne and he was brought back to our planet, where he showed us the futility of our hitherto peaceful but boring life of study.'

'You have six of your Earth hours to find and deliver the fugitives,' boomed Tarduz.

'Or you will be vaporised,' said Zigg.

'Vaporised?' said Sponge with a whimper.

'Vaporised!' confirmed the aliens with an evil-sounding cackle.

# 11 Ants from Outer Space

The boys got back in record time, sliding and scrabbling down the bracken-swathed slopes of Pug's Peak and rushing, gasping like beached mackerel, into school. They were almost glad to have the familiar noxious fumes of lunch assault their quivering nostrils. By the time they reached the dorm, this slap to the senses had revived them a little.

'Well, I'm for making a run for it,' said Kenningworth, packing his trunk. 'Who's with me?'

'Run where?' said Mildew. 'They said they were going to vaporise the planet.'

Kenningworth stopped his frantic packing.

'Oh – yes,' he said glumly. 'That does make escape a trifle difficult. We need to find those criminal aliens and we need to find them fast.'

The boys nodded.

'But how?' said Sponge. 'They could be anywhere. And we don't even know what they look like.'

'Or what size they are,' said Filbert.

'Size?' said Mildew. 'What difference does that make?'

'Well, they could be tiny,' said Filbert. 'You know – like ants.'

The boys instinctively looked down at the floor.

'They may actually be ants,' said Hipflask.

'Are you saying that ants are aliens or that these particular aliens are ants from outer space?' asked Furthermore.

Hipflask shrugged.

'Either,' he said. 'Or both. Or neither.'

Furthermore rolled his eyes.

'Or they could be huge,' said Footstool, 'and scary.'

'Scarier than those giant mechanical spiders?' said Kenningworth. 'Unlikely. Plus we'd have noticed them by now if they were. The scariest thing round here is Mrs Glump's cooking. If there are aliens about, why haven't we seen them?'

'Yes,' said Furthermore. 'Surely we'd have noticed. The likelihood is they will be very different from us. They could just be some kind of floating blob for all we know.'

Mildew and Sponge had the same thought at exactly the same moment.

'Giant floating eyeballs!' they said in unison.

'What?' said the other boys.

Mildew and Sponge were remembering their encounter with a giant floating eyeball on their trip into the near future in the time machine. Surely the giant floating eyeball must be one of the renegade aliens the Neenor were looking for.

'Er … We just thought the aliens might be giant floating eyeballs,' said Mildew. 'Just a wild guess.'

'That's quite specific,' said Furthermore.

Mildew and Sponge opened their respective mouths but only air made any attempt to come out.

'Why are we listening to these cough drops anyway?' said Kenningworth. 'Have you forgotten we are in imminent danger of being vaporised?'

'And what was all that about Stupendo being the Great One?' said Furthermore. 'How could Stupendo be around at the time of the dinosaurs? It makes no sense.'

Mildew and Sponge shrugged and adopted an expression they felt sure conveyed a complete lack of knowledge of all Stupendo-related matters. Kenningworth peered at them suspiciously.

'I wonder if we shouldn't tell the teachers,' said Mildew, backing away from him.

'The teachers?' said Kenningworth. 'Wouldn't they just get in the way? We're trying to speed things up.'

'Sponge and I have had reason to consult Mr Luckless on a number of occasions in recent weeks, on a variety of subjects. He has proved to be very sensible and useful.'

'Are we talking about the same Mr Luckless?' said Kenningworth. 'The twitchy history teacher who would jump at his own shadow?'

'That's a little unfair,' said Sponge.

'Let's all go and see him now,' said Hipflask. 'We have to do *something*.'

'No,' said Mildew. 'I think it's best Sponge and I see him alone. A crowd of us will make him even more nervous than he usually is. He's easily flustered.'

'And yet Mr Luckless is the one we're pinning our hopes on?' said Kenningworth.

'All right. Go and see what he says,' said Furthermore. 'We'll wait for you in the refectory.'

'The refectory?' said Mildew. 'Surely you can't eat at a time like this?'

'I'm hungry,' said Furthermore.

'Me too,' said Enderpenny.

'Come on, Sponge,' said Mildew.

'But I'm also hungry,' said Sponge.

Mildew was already heading towards Mr Luckless's classroom, though, and after only the minutest of pauses, Sponge set off after him.

*T*he boys found Mr Luckless, the history teacher, in his classroom. Peering through the window in his door, they saw he was in his usual state of dreamy melancholy.

This had become the norm ever since the Roman love of his life, Miss Livia – brought to Maudlin Towers during Mr Luckless's own time-travelling adventures – had returned to her own time (and husband).

'Poor Mr Luckless,' said Sponge. 'It seems as though he will never recover from the loss of Miss Livia.'

Mildew nodded.

'In many ways his behaviour is similar to that of Miss Bronteen's,' he replied. 'Who can understand the ways of teachers, Sponge?'

After several knocks, Mr Luckless snapped out of his despond enough to respond, and bade them enter.

'Ah, boys,' he said, frowning slightly and with an air of trepidation that did not go unnoticed.

'Is everything all right, sir?' asked Mildew. 'You don't seem entirely pleased to see us.'

Mr Luckless laced his fingers together and eased himself back into his chair. His lips pouted and twitched beneath his moustache as though struggling to give form to his thoughts.

'Hmmm,' he said. 'Well. Let me see. How can I put this? There does seem to be an unfortunate pattern forming.'

'A pattern, sir?' said Sponge. 'How so?'

Mr Luckless sighed and pushed his spectacles back up the bridge of his nose.

'Well, I don't want to seem churlish, boys, but you only come and see me when something bad has happened or is about to happen. Or,' he added, nervously peering through the open door behind them, 'when something bad is actually already happening.'

'Oh, that can't be true,' said Mildew. He tried, but failed, however, to think of an occasion where this had not been the case.

'Well?' said Mr Luckless.

'Sir?'

'Has something bad happened?' he asked. 'Or is something bad about to happen? Or is it already happening?'

'Erm ...' began Mildew. 'When you put it like that, yes.'

'Which?' said Mr Luckless.

'Both,' said Sponge. 'All.'

Mr Luckless made a slight whining noise through his nose.

'Out with it then,' he said.

Mildew looked at Sponge. Sponge looked at Mildew. They both looked at Mr Luckless. There didn't seem any way to ease into it, so they decided it was best to blurt it out.

'We have been invaded by creatures from another world, sir.'

Mr Luckless paused a moment and then chuckled heartily. Mildew raised an eyebrow and stared at Sponge, who shrugged in befuddlement. Mr Luckless chuckled on.

'You don't seem overly concerned, sir,' said Mildew.

'Oh, boys, boys,' he said, wiping a tear from his eye. 'They may seem like creatures from another world but the fairer sex are the same as us. Well, not exactly the same as us, of course …'

Mr Luckless blushed at his own words. The boys accompanied him for a moment.

'Not the girls, sir,' said Mildew with a sigh. 'Actual creatures from an actual other world. Aliens, if you will.'

'But what do you mean?' said Mr Luckless. 'Don't tell me the Belgians have landed!'

'No, sir – this is a vehicular craft from …'

The boys both pointed upwards and Mr Luckless could not help but follow their gaze – and found himself examining the light fitting.

'From the lower school's English department's stock cupboard?'

'From the heavens, sir,' said Sponge. 'Not from upstairs.'

'But such things are only the fanciful imaginings of fantastical fiction ...'

Mildew pulled out the drawing he had done up on Pug's Peak and carefully placed it in front of the history teacher. Mr Luckless stared in amazement and got to his feet, his chair screeching on the floor like a wounded squid.

'Good Lord!' he cried.

'There's more, sir,' said Mildew. 'Be brave. It involves Mr Stupendo.'

'Mr Stupendo?' said Mr Luckless, collapsing back into his seat. 'Our old sports teacher? He's not back, is he? I never really liked –'

'The fact is, sir,' said Mildew, 'Sponge and I may have sent him back to the time of the dinosaurs ...'

Mr Luckless put his hand to his head in astonishment but then chuckled despite himself.

'The poor man,' said Mr Luckless. 'Or should we say, poor dinosaurs!'

'Very droll, sir,' said Mildew. 'Sadly these very same creatures from another world also came here at that very same dawn of time and took said sports teacher to their planet where they seem to have worshipped him like some kind of hairless-headed god. They call him the Great One.'

'The Great One?'

They nodded solemnly.

'Good grief,' said Mr Luckless.

'This is all because of Mr Particle's time machine, sir,' said Mildew. 'It has caused mayhem.'

'I think it's best we keep the time machine to ourselves, boys,' said Mr Luckless with an arch of the eyebrow. 'But we really do have to inform the Headmaster of this current crisis.'

'Very well, sir,' said Mildew.

'I'm glad you came to me, boys,' said Mr Luckless, getting to his feet. 'I'm glad you saw me as someone you could put your faith in.'

'So are we, sir,' they said.

'Aaargh!' cried Mr Luckless, jumping sideways.

The boys did likewise, looking around in horror to see what it was that had terrified their teacher.

'Ah – it's all right,' he said. 'Panic over. Just my own shadow.'

Mildew and Sponge glanced at each other, sighed and followed their history teacher out of the room.

13 Miss Pernickety

Mr Luckless and the boys strode through cloister and corridor until they came to the Headmaster's office. Mr Luckless rapped on the door and after a moment Miss Pernickety unbolted and unlocked it, opening it only very slightly.

'Mr Luckless?' she said, peering suspiciously through the crack. 'Can I help you?'

'We are here to see the Headmaster.'

'I'm very sorry,' said Miss Pernickety, closing the door. 'The Headmaster is busy.'

'But this is urgent,' said Mr Luckless, trying to force the door open again.

'The Headmaster is busy,' growled Miss Pernickety, putting her shoulder against the door and pushing Mr Luckless back.

'To me, boys,' said Mr Luckless. 'Miss Pernickety is surprisingly strong.'

Mildew and Sponge added their weight to Mr Luckless's and they burst through the door into the office and set off towards the Headmaster's study.

But before Mr Luckless could place his hand on the door handle, Miss Pernickety leaped like a panther on to his back, grabbing him round the neck and wailing like a banshee.

'The Headmaster is busy!!!' she yelled.

Mr Luckless staggered round and round, choking, with Miss Pernickety whirling about, her feet scattering things this way and that. Mr Luckless turned the colour of boiled ham, his eyes bulging.

Mildew tried to intervene but was caught round the side of the head by Miss Pernickety's foot, knocking him high into the air to land on top of a filing cabinet.

'What is the meaning of this?' said the Headmaster, suddenly standing in the doorway.

Mr Luckless came to a halt with Miss Pernickety still tied around his neck like a jumper. Sponge helped Mildew down from the filing cabinet.

'I told him you were busy but he would not listen, Headmaster.'

'Very well, my dear,' said the Headmaster. 'You did your best. I shall take it from here.'

'Yes, Headmaster,' she said, releasing her grip and dropping to the floor with a gentle thud. She straightened her clothes and returned to her desk as though nothing had happened.

'Miss Pernickety takes her secretarial duties very seriously, doesn't she, Headmaster?' said Mr Luckless as he followed him to his study, rubbing his throat.

'Oh yes,' said the Headmaster. 'You are lucky to be alive.'

Mr Luckless chuckled at this but the Headmaster turned to face him and they saw that it was no joke. Sponge looked back at Miss Pernickety and hurried on. When they entered the study they found the Headmistress of the girls' school sitting in an armchair.

'You have company,' said Mr Luckless.

'I told you he was busy!' bellowed Miss Pernickety from the other room.

'I don't think you've been introduced,' said the Headmaster. 'Mr Luckless, this is Miss MT2T.'

'Miss MT2T?' said Mr Luckless. 'What an unusual name. Is it Scottish perhaps?'

'I do not ... have sufficient information ... to answer that ... question.'

'I see,' said Mr Luckless.

'How is it ... that you are ... doing?' said Miss MT2T.

'I am very well, thank you,' said Mr Luckless. 'I trust that you have been made to feel welcome in Maudlin Towers.'

'There have been ... no outward signs ... of hostility,' said Miss MT2T.

'Ah, excellent,' said Mr Luckless. 'Frankly, that would go down as a good day for me.'

'Have you seen Mr Gruntforth at all?' said the Headmaster.

'Mr Gruntforth?' said Mr Luckless. 'No, Headmaster.'

'Haven't laid eyes on him since he decided to go on a jog up Pug's Peak this morning.'

The boys and Mr Luckless exchanged a glance. It sounded like the Headmaster would be recruiting yet another sports master …

'You had something urgent to tell me,' said the Headmaster to Mr Luckless.

'Yes,' replied the history teacher, casting a glance at Miss MT2T. 'I wonder if I shouldn't wait until –'

'I will leave now,' said Miss MT2T.

'Must you?' said the Headmaster. 'But I was so looking forward to showing you my shoe collection. Another time, then.'

Miss MT2T left the room, accompanied by the faintest clanking and hissing.

'Now what was so important that you had to risk your life in mortal combat with Miss Pernickety?'

'Sir,' said Mr Luckless. 'The boys have terrible news.'

'Well, it had better be terrible, for your sakes,' said the Headmaster.

Sponge whimpered.

'We have been invaded by creatures from another world!' cried Mildew.

The Headmaster smiled and opened his mouth to speak.

'Not the girls!' cried Mr Luckless, Mildew and Sponge in unison.

'But surely there is some mistake,' said the Headmaster. 'This is the stuff of fiction. You have become far too influenced by those Vernon Jules fantasies you read, Mr Luckless.'

'Show him, Mildew.'

Mildew pulled out his drawing and showed it to the Headmaster, who staggered backwards.

'Good Lord!' he cried. 'It can't be.'

'And yet it is, sir,' said Mildew.

'What on earth do they want?'

'They say they are looking for some renegade criminals. They have informed us they will vaporise the planet if we don't hand them over. In six hours.'

'Six hours!' cried the Headmaster.

'Actually, it's more like five now,' said Sponge.

'But surely we would have noticed if alien criminals had arrived at Maudlin Towers,' said the Headmaster. 'How can we hand them over if we do not have them? It's outrageous. They have clearly made a mistake. I'm sure they'll see reason.'

'They don't look like the kind of giant mechanical spiders who go in for reason that much, sir,' said Mildew.

'Spiders?'

'Yes, they are called Zigg and Tarduz and they are spiders from Marzz.'

'Mars?' said the Headmaster.

'No, sir – Marzz,' said Sponge. 'A different place entirely, apparently.'

'Gather the staff!' said the Headmaster to Mr Luckless. 'We shall go and parley with these creatures. I refuse to be threatened or bullied! That's *my* job!'

# 14
## For Maudlin Towers!

The Headmaster gathered the staff together in the school hall. The boys of Maudlin Towers were present too and the visiting girls, who stood in another bustling group overseen by Miss MT2T. It was a bit of a squeeze.

'What ... is ... occurring?' said Miss MT2T.

'Please do not concern yourself, madam,' said the Headmaster. 'Everything will be resolved shortly.'

There was a great deal of muttering and mumbling until the Headmaster nodded to the Reverend Brimstone, who bellowed at everyone to be silent or risk eternal torment, his eyes swivelling like spinning billiard balls.

'Thank you, Reverend,' said the Headmaster. 'Well put as always. If I could have your attention.'

Miss Bronteen opened her mouth to speak but a quick growl from Reverend Brimstone silenced her once more.

'Maudlin Towers is in mortal danger,' said the Headmaster.

There were gasps from the staff and pupils alike. The Headmaster raised his hands.

'Mortal danger?' said Flintlock, the groundsman. 'Shall I fetch the school cannon, Headmaster?'

'Maybe later,' replied the Headmaster. 'Let's try reason first.'

'Have I ever told you,' began Mr Drumlin, the geography teacher, 'about the time I was surrounded by the –'

'Yes!' shouted the staff.

'With nothing to staunch the flames but my own –'

'Yes!'

'But what on earth is going on, Headmaster?' said Mr Riddell, the art teacher. 'I have an allegorical etching to window-mount.'

'I will explain everything,' said the Headmaster. 'Although it may stretch your powers of understanding to their twanging point. I myself took some persuading. But these two brave boys have informed me that Maudlin Towers – or at least its environs – has been invaded by creatures from another world!'

There was a pause of several moments before raucous chuckling broke out among the staff. The Headmaster's smile began to falter and he turned to Reverend Brimstone for support, only to find he was among the most enthusiastic of the chucklers.

'Show them, Mildew!' demanded the Head-master.

Mildew nodded, and brought out his drawing, showing it to each of the staff in turn. Reverend Brimstone was the last to see it and the last to stop chuckling, but when he did, he dropped to his knees in prayer, gibbering like a puzzled dormouse.

'*Mon Dieu!*' cried Miss Bleu. 'It iz true!'

The room descended into a clamour of anxious jabbering before the Headmaster called on Reverend Brimstone to bellow the crowd into silence for a second time.

'These creatures say they are in pursuit of criminals and they believe that these criminals are here, in Maudlin Towers. They demand we hand them over or the entire planet will be vaporised.'

'But how can we hand them over if we do not have them, Headmaster?' asked Miss Bronteen.

'Precisely,' said the Headmaster. 'That is the perilous pickle we now find ourselves in.'

The staff broke out into another chorus of jabbering.

'Enough! The planet needs us. More importantly, the school needs us!' cried the Headmaster. 'And when our school needs us, we answer its call. We do not ask what may become of us –'

'Don't we?' asked Mr Luckless.

'No!' said the Headmaster. 'We simply stride forth and do our duty. These boys may not be very bright, nor their parents very rich, but they have been placed in our care and we will do everything we can to protect them.

'And chance has also made us guardians to these girls, who find themselves among us, and we shall defend them as steadfastly as any of our boys. For we are teachers – teachers! – and there is no nobler or finer calling. We are teachers and we know no fear! Come, comrades. For Maudlin Towers!'

'For Maudlin Towers!' cried the staff.

'I … insist … that I … accompany … you,' said Miss MT2T.

'By Jove,' said the Headmaster. 'I like your spirit,

I must say. We will be honoured to have you in our ranks.'

'But what is it that we hope to achieve, Headmaster?' said Mr Luckless, some of his resolve already deserting him.

'We shall appeal to their sense of reason,' said the Headmaster with a smile. 'I'm sure there has simply been a terrible misunderstanding. Perhaps a problem with translation.'

'Bravo, sir,' said Mildew as the Headmaster began to stride away. 'Very stirring. I may make a note or two to that effect in my diary. Should you fail to return I shall ensure the governors have a very –'

'No, no, no,' said the Headmaster. 'We will need you as guides. Come along.'

'But, sir,' protested Mildew. 'My knees …'

'Show some Maudlin grit, Mildew,' said the Headmaster. 'What would your father say?'

'"Run", I imagine,' said Mildew.

'Be that as it may, you're coming with us. And you, Spongely-Partwork.'

The two boys groaned and hung their heads, but the Headmaster would not be dissuaded.

'Ha!' cried Kenningworth.

'You too, Kenningworth!' said the Headmaster over his shoulder.

'Why me, sir?' said Kenningworth.

'A Maudlin boy never asks why, Kenningworth, only what!'

'What?' said Kenningworth.

'Good man!' said the Headmaster.

Kenningworth muttered and Mildew and Sponge trudged along behind him as he followed the Headmaster out of the school and up the hill.

'All will be well,' said Mr Luckless, smiling at the boys.

'You seem oddly confident all of a sudden, sir,' said Mildew. 'Given the giant mechanical spiders and so forth. I should have expected you to be more concerned.'

Mr Luckless leaned forward and whispered.

'I'll let you in on a secret. Do you remember when I had the time machine and was taking Miss Livia back to Roman times?'

'When her husband gave you the black eye?' said Mildew.

'Quite,' said Mr Luckless with a frown. 'Moving on … Well, I overshot my return and ended up in the future.'

'How far in the future, sir?' said Sponge.

'I don't know entirely but it can't be too far from now – and all was well.'

'Well, that's a relief,' said Sponge.

'How did you know?' said Mildew. 'How could you be sure that all was well?'

'Because you told me, Mildew,' said Mr Luckless with a smile. 'I asked you how things were and you said, "Everything is back to normal."'

'Stop talking in the ranks!' yelled the Headmaster, making Mr Luckless jump.

Eventually they reached the summit of Pug's Peak and found it deserted. The Headmaster strode forward towards the alien space-carriage with all the authority he could muster.

'Hello?' he cried. 'Hello? I demand to speak to whomever is in charge!'

'Do you have the alien criminals?' boomed a voice Mildew and Sponge recognised as Tarduz.

'No,' said the Headmaster. 'But –'

'Then you are wasting time,' boomed Zigg. 'Go away!'

'Well said, old planet,' said Tarduz.

'We will not go away!' said the Headmaster.

The rest of the teachers cheered in agreement. Reverend Brimstone stepped forward, growling.

'If you aren't going to look for the aliens you are of no use to us,' boomed Tarduz.

'Now see here!' cried the Headmaster. 'You can't just –'

A crackling beam of light burst from the alien craft and, separating out into smaller tentacle-like beams, hit each member of staff in turn, including Miss MT2T, lifting them off the ground and leaving them dangling four feet in the air.

# 15. Not Cricket

Mildew, Sponge and Kenningworth stared in amazement at their dangling teachers. They seemed frozen, eyes open but oblivious, like floating statues or hovering uncles. Kenningworth reached up and gave Miss Bronteen a shove, making her dance like a lantern.

'Who are you?' said Tarduz, emerging from the alien craft and pointing one of its long metal feet at Kenningworth.

'Er … Kenningworth. I was here earlier. For the record I didn't really want to come back.'

'Who are these slightly larger Earthlings who now dangle before us?' said Zigg, lumbering forward too. 'And why are they so annoying?'

'The answer to the first question is they are our teachers,' said Kenningworth. 'Which is also the answer to your second question.'

'Then we shall vaporise them!' cried Tarduz.

'No!' shouted Mildew.

'But you find them as annoying as we do,' said Zigg. 'It's obvious. What is your problem?'

'Maybe so,' said Mildew. 'Maybe they are annoying. Sometimes. Often. But you can't just go round vaporising everything that annoys you.'

'Why not?' said Zigg.

'Yes – why not, Mildew?' said Kenningworth.

'Why not?' said Mildew. 'Why not? Tell him, Sponge.'

'Because it's not cricket,' said Sponge.

'Explain cricket,' said Tarduz.

'No one can explain cricket,' said Mildew.

'The Great One spoke of cricket,' said Zigg. 'It is a thing of wonder and beauty, more exciting and meaningful than life itself.'

'Are you sure he was talking about cricket?' said Kenningworth.

'We need more information,' said Zigg.

The suction cups snaked out again and plonked down on to the heads of Mildew and Sponge.

'Not interested in reading my mind, then?' said Kenningworth. 'Not that I care.'

'We only have the two. Sorry.'

Kenningworth rolled his eyes and tutted. A few seconds later Mildew and Sponge were released and the boys fell down dizzily. The mechanical spiders clanked and wheezed, staggering a little.

'We learned almost nothing at all about this so-called cricket of yours,' said Zigg.

'We told you,' said Mildew, getting up slowly. 'It's impossible to –'

'The small one seems to think of nothing but biscuits and the larger one about something called Felicity Fallowfield.'

Mildew blushed. Sponge grinned. Kenningworth snorted.

'Let's go a little deeper this time,' said Tarduz.

The suction cups plopped back on to the

boys' heads. Once again Mildew and Sponge slumped dizzily to the ground as the cups were pulled away.

'You won't find anything in there,' said Kenningworth. 'You'd find more in an empty bin.'

'On the contrary,' boomed Zigg. 'We learned about bearded creatures with horned helmets, women from the period you call "Roman" and men who turn into wolves …'

'Really?' said Kenningworth. 'Are you sure those things aren't faulty?'

'Most important of all, we learned about the time machine!'

'The what?' said Kenningworth.

'The time machine?' said Mildew. 'I'm not sure I quite follow? Are you talking about a clock? There are several of those around the –'

'You know exactly what we are talking about!' boomed Zigg. 'We demand that you hand over the criminals – and your time machine.'

'Not necessarily in that order,' said Tarduz.

'Shhhh. Let me do the talking,' said Zigg.

'I was just trying to help,' said Tarduz.

'I know that, old star,' said Zigg.

'What are they talking about, Mildew?' said Kenningworth. 'We don't have a time machine.'

'See!' said Mildew. 'There you are! We don't have one.'

'And besides,' said Sponge. 'You wouldn't fit in it. You're too big.'

'Sponge!' hissed Mildew.

'Ah – the prickly-headed one thinks these are our actual forms,' said Zigg.

There was a faint beeping, a series of whinnying noises, a clunk and then, after a pause, a hollow bong, and then out from the glowing orbs atop the spidery bodies came two smaller orbs which floated towards the startled boys. Inside each was a brain.

'Urgh,' said Kenningworth.

'You see,' said Zigg, 'we are not too big. We have evolved beyond your need for a body. We have no need for food. Or your Earthly trousers.'

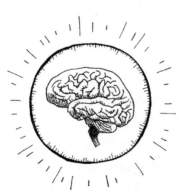

'I miss food,' said Tarduz.

'Me too,' said Zigg. 'Especially biscuits – but we should talk about this later, old moon.'

107

'Oh – yes – probably.'

'Find those criminals now and bring us your time machine!'

'What exactly have these criminals done, anyway?' asked Kenningworth.

'Something terrible,' said Zigg in a trembling voice. 'A crime of such enormity it would make your blood run cold if I told you.'

'All the same,' said Kenningworth, 'why can't you get them yourselves?'

'Because they are blocking our scanners. They are cunning. We know they are here but we cannot find them.'

'Then how do you expect us to find them?'

'That is your problem,' said Zigg. 'We could just have vaporised you from the start. But because the Great One believed in fair play we are giving you a sporting chance.'

'No, you're not,' said Kenningworth.

'Enough! To ensure you keep to the task, Kevin here will be keeping an eye on you, as it were …' Zigg chuckled.

'Good one,' said Tarduz. 'That never gets old.'

'I know,' said Zigg. 'Kevin! Get a move on.'

Out from their craft popped the very same giant floating eyeball Sponge and Mildew had seen only a few weeks earlier when they had travelled to a few weeks later in the time machine.

'Aaaargh!' cried Sponge.

'Aaaargh!' seconded Mildew.

'Aaaargh!' cried Kenningworth.

The boys left their dangling teachers behind and beat a hasty retreat down the side of Pug's Peak, Kevin the giant floating eyeball bobbing eerily along over the bracken in pursuit.

# 16 The Bothy

The boys slithered down the side of the hill and were just pausing for breath outside the bothy when Kenningworth turned to Mildew and Sponge and peered at them until they both backed away.

'Are you quite all right?' said Mildew. 'Only you seem a tad agitated.'

'What was all that about time machines?' said Kenningworth.

'That?' said Mildew, looking round to check if Kevin was there. 'Oh – you know aliens, always talking nonsense. The way they do. Aliens. Tell him, Sponge.'

Kenningworth peered at Sponge. Sponge's mouth swung open like a door in a light summer breeze and then swung shut again. The shadow of

Kevin fell over them for a moment but the eyeball
floated past across the sports field.

'You look like you're hiding something, Sponge,'
said Kenningworth.

Sponge whimpered.

'Oh, Sponge always looks like that,' said Mildew.
'That's basically Sponge's look. That's classic
Sponge.'

'What's going on?' said Kenningworth.

'Going on?' said Mildew. 'Going on?'

'Yes – going on. With you two. What are you
up to?'

'Up to?' said Mildew.

'Stop just repeating what I'm saying,' said
Kenningworth. 'You know what I mean. You've
seen that giant floating eyeball before, haven't you?'

'Er …' murmured Sponge, looking at Mildew.

'Well, I suppose at least we know the alien criminals aren't giant floating eyeballs,' said Mildew.

'But that means we still don't know who they actually are!' said Sponge.

'True,' said Mildew.

'Look – come on,' said Kenningworth. 'What is all this about – men in horned helmets, Romans and werewolves and time machines? We haven't got time for secrets.'

Mildew and Sponge looked at each other.

'Tell me, you dog biscuits,' insisted Kenningworth.

'All right!' said Mildew. 'It's true. There was a time machine.'

'Don't tell him, Mildew,' said Sponge.

'Er … he just has,' said Kenningworth. 'Continue …'

Mildew sighed.

'It was Mr Particle who invented it,' he said.

'The physics teacher?' said Kenningworth. 'The dead one?'

'How many Mr Particles do you know?' said Mildew. 'Anyway. He invented a time machine and went back and forth in time and so on.'

'Where is this so-called time machine of Particle's? How come none of us ever saw it and you have?'

'As a matter of fact, it was in here,' said Sponge. 'In the bothy.'

Kenningworth put his hand on the door latch.

'There's nothing there now, of course,' said Mildew as Kenningworth opened the door with a creak.

'No,' said Kenningworth. 'You're right. Just this old armchair with a load of junk stuck to it for some reason.'

Mildew and Sponge rushed forward.

'The time machine!' they cried. 'It's back!'

'What?' said Kenningworth. 'That thing? You're trying to tell me that flea-bitten old armchair with clock dials and levers is a time machine? I don't believe you.'

'Well, it's true,' said Mildew.

'Prove it,' said Kenningworth.

'We don't need to prove it,' said Mildew. Kenningworth strode over and flopped down in the time machine. Mildew and Sponge rushed forward to try and pull him out.

'Let go of me!' cried Kenningworth. 'You've both gone stark raving –'

In his struggles to free himself of Mildew's grip, Kenningworth reached out a hand and grabbed a lever, yanking it back and causing the all too familiar dizzying effects of time travel.

'– mad,' said Kenningworth.

'Look what you've done!' said Mildew. 'We don't even know whether we've gone forwards or backwards, or for how long.'

'What are you talking about?' said Kenningworth. 'Everything is exactly the same.'

Kenningworth did seem to have a point. The interior of the bothy did seem almost identical. Almost. The more they looked the more they felt that while it was still a damp and filthy collection of mould and dust and cobwebs, it was as though everything was rather more artfully arranged than before. As though the untidiness was just a little too neat.

Mildew and Sponge let go of Kenningworth and he stood up and walked over to the door, opening it and looking out. There was Maudlin Towers, just the same as ever … except that somehow, like the bothy, the cloud-swaddled spires and pinnacles seemed crisper, their points sharper, their gargoyles more distinct, more clearly defined.

'I think it would be best if we went straight back,' said Sponge.

'Back to what?' said Kenningworth. 'Back to a couple of deranged mechanical spiders and imminent vaporisation?'

'Strictly speaking,' said Mildew, 'we might have to go forward rather than back.'

'Precisely,' said Kenningworth. 'We need more information.'

'But –'

'Oh, it's all right for you, you flannels,' said Kenningworth. 'You've had a go in this before. Can't I just have one small glimpse?'

Mildew leaned towards the time machine and peered at the dials.

'I think we've gone into the future,' said Mildew. 'I think the best thing to do is –'

'He's gone,' said Sponge.

'Well, why didn't you try to stop him?' said Mildew.

The boys stood at the open door of the bothy but Kenningworth was nowhere to be seen.

'We could just leave him here,' said Mildew.

The two boys gave this some thought until Sponge shook his head.

'No, Mildew,' he said. 'We can't. This is Kenningworth. It's not fair to whatever period we've arrived in. Who knows what he might do. Besides – it's our fault. If we hadn't sent Stupendo back, none of this would have happened.'

Mildew heaved a heartfelt sigh and nodded.

'I suppose you're right,' he said. 'Come on, then ...'

# Back to the Future Maudlin Towers

Mildew and Sponge set off towards the school, heading along the ha-ha next to the sports field. After some discussion about where to start their search, they decided to enter through the main door and see if they might ascertain which period they were in. As soon as they were inside, it became clear.

'It's the same bit of the future we came to before,' said Mildew. 'One hundred and fifty years ahead. Look – the Headmaster's office is full of jigsaws and jam again.'

'And expensive biscuits,' said Sponge.

'But where on earth is Kenningworth?' said Mildew. 'And how are we going to find him?'

'Hello!' said a voice behind them.

There stood a girl clad all in black, peering at

them sullenly from under her fringe. She pointed a black-painted fingernail at them.

'You've come back.'

'I'm sorry,' said Mildew. 'I think you must be mistaking us for someone else.'

'Oh no,' said the girl. 'You disappeared in a time machine about ten minutes ago. My dad is Tweeting about it.'

'He's doing what?' said Sponge.

Then both boys remembered at once. This girl was here the last time they came. Her family was in Mr Luckless's classroom, and later they also witnessed Mildew and Sponge's departure from the bothy.

'Ah,' said Mildew. 'It wasn't a real time machine, of course.'

'You disappeared,' said the girl.

'It's just an illusion,' said Mildew. 'It's all done with mirrors.'

'No, it isn't,' said the girl. 'You're from the past, just like you said.'

'Run, Sponge!' hissed Mildew.

The two boys scurried as fast as their feeble

calves would carry them, and although she attempted to follow, their knowledge of the layout of Maudlin Towers was vastly superior despite the passage of time.

Once they felt sure they had given her the slip, they did a brisk tour of the school, checking in each room for any sign of Kenningworth, but at the close of this extensive search no sign was forthcoming.

'We need to get back,' said Mildew. 'Before we attract any more unwanted attention.'

'Maybe Kenningworth went back to the bothy to find us,' said Sponge.

'Good thought,' said Mildew. 'It's worth a try.'

The two friends hurried back out of the school. Sponge noticed a sign saying CAR PARK.

'I wonder what a car is?' said Sponge.

'Well, we haven't got time to –'

To their amazement they saw that the entire upper sports field was full of coloured metal carriages, some of which were moving about without the aid of even a single horse.

'Sponge,' said Mildew. 'Are you seeing what I'm seeing?'

Sponge nodded. One of the carriages – of a particularly cruel shade of green – drove straight towards them and the boys headed off to the relative safety of the ha-ha and the bothy.

But when they burst inside they found that their day was about to get worse.

'It's not there!' said Mildew, stating the obvious.

The time machine was no longer there.

'Kenningworth must have come back and left without us,' said Mildew.

'The blot,' said Sponge. 'How could he?'

'Because he's a blot, Sponge,' said Mildew.

They stared in disbelief at the empty space, their minds unable to come to terms with the enormity of their predicament.

'We're marooned here,' said Sponge.

'Meanwhile Kenningworth is hurtling about in the time machine,' said Mildew. 'Who knows what he might do if he heads into the past.'

'I suppose we'd know about it if he'd done something really bad,' said Sponge.

'Would we?' said Mildew. 'It's not as though terrible things haven't happened in the past. Who knows whether Kenningworth was behind any of them. He could have started the Black Death or invented maths for all we know.'

Sponge nodded. Maths was just the kind of thing a blot like Kenningworth would come up with.

'And how can we stay here?' said Mildew. 'It's madness out there. We won't last a minute. Look at the price of biscuits for one thing.'

The mention of biscuits was too much for Sponge.

'I knew he didn't like us,' said Sponge tearfully. 'But to just leave us here like this. I wouldn't have believed even he would do that.'

Suddenly the door to the bothy swung open and there stood Kenningworth.

'Ah,' said Mildew. 'We were just talking about you, weren't we?'

'Yes,' said Sponge.

'I know,' said Kenningworth, frowning. 'I heard.'

Mildew and Sponge exchanged a glance but Kenningworth spoke first.

'Where's the time machine? Given that I didn't take it.'

'Sorry,' said Mildew. 'It's just that –'

'It's just that I'm a blot,' said Kenningworth. 'Yes – I know. But where is it?'

'We don't know.'

Kenningworth kicked out at the door.

'Who would have taken it?' he said. 'Who even knew it was here?'

Mildew and Sponge sighed as they realised it must be the black-clad girl they had bumped into. She must have run to the bothy either to find them or simply to have a go in what she knew to be a time machine.

'It's a girl from this time,' said Mildew. 'She saw us on the last visit here and we met again.'

'You've been here before?'

They nodded.

'But this place is utter madness,' said Kenningworth. 'There are people talking to themselves holding what look like oblong coasters to their heads.'

Mildew and Sponge nodded.

'Makes you wonder what the point of it all is if this is what the world is destined for. Say what you like about the Maudlin of our time, but at least it –'

'But don't you see?' said Mildew suddenly. 'If Maudlin Towers is here, even in this bizarre form, it means the planet hasn't been vaporised, which must mean we defeat the Neenor. Somehow.'

'Or the other fellows do,' said Kenningworth. 'Or the girls. We might not play any part at all.'

The three boys sighed.

'Well, I'm glad they were beaten, whoever did it,' said Sponge.

'Agreed,' said Mildew.

'Agreed,' said Kenningworth, after a pause.

18

A Moving Talking Painting

They had a brief discussion about what was the best course of action and the only thing they could think of was to find the family of the black-clad girl and try to enlist them in the attempt to bring her back. They all agreed they could not simply stand there staring at the space vacated by the time machine.

The boys set off towards the school, attracting friendly attention from an elderly couple they passed.

'Isn't it lovely how they've dressed these children up to look like they're from olden times?' said the women as they passed by.

'Everyone assumes we're actors,' said Mildew. 'Just like when we were last here.'

They thought it best to stick together in case

splitting up simply resulted in more confusion if the girl did suddenly appear. They were just looking in the hall when they saw a group of people seated in front of what looked like a large painting. Except that it was moving and also, apparently, talking.

One minute it showed pictures of Maudlin Towers from high above, as though from a balloon or from the viewpoint of one of the many ravens that croaked their way over the crags of Pig's Pike, the next it showed a painting of Lord Marzipan Maudlin, and then, to their amazement, it showed a classroom photograph from the time when it was Maudlin Towers School for the Not Particularly Bright Sons of the Not Especially Wealthy.

'What is this?' said Kenningworth. 'I feel dizzy.'

'That's us,' said Sponge. 'That's us in the past.'

'Hello,' said a voice behind them.

The three boys turned to see the black-clad girl.

'You!' said Mildew. 'Where's our time machine?'

'Back where you left it,' she said. 'Apparently it's really important that you get back.'

'Who told you that?' said Kenningworth.

'He did,' said the girl, pointing at Mildew.

'How did you find us?' said Sponge.

'He said you'd be in the school hall looking baffled in front of the talking painting. And here

you are. It's called a television, by the way.'

Kenningworth and Sponge turned to Mildew, who shrugged.

'I haven't said it yet,' he protested. 'I don't know what she's talking about.'

'Anyway,' she said. 'I'm sorry I took it without permission. It was pretty cool though.'

'It's always a bit chilly in Maudlin Towers,' said Mildew.

'Looked like quite a lot of stuff was going on,' she said with a sigh. 'Not like here. It's sooooo boring here.'

'It's mostly boring in our time, too,' said Mildew. 'Honest.'

'Yes,' said Sponge. 'I'd say ninety-per-cent boredom.'

'Ninety-five easily,' said Kenningworth. 'Maybe even ninety-eight.'

'You just happened to arrive when there were floating eyeballs and aliens and such,' said Mildew.

The black-clad girl nodded.

'Thank you for rescuing us,' said Mildew.

'You're welcome, I suppose,' she said. 'Bye, then.'

'Farewell,' said Mildew.

Then she leaned forward and kissed Mildew on the cheek, causing him to blush and wheeze.

'Sorry,' she said with a crooked smile. 'Couldn't resist. Just to see the look on your face again.'

'Again?' said Sponge, outraged.

She gave them a wave and then turned with another great sigh, and walked away, head bowed.

Kenningworth was fiddling with a long, black oblong covered in small buttons with numbers and symbols on them.

'What is it?' said Sponge.

'I don't know,' said Kenningworth. 'It was near the moving painting. I saw a woman point it at it to change the picture.'

130

Kenningworth pointed it at the real Maudlin Towers and tapped the buttons.

'No!' cried Mildew.

But nothing happened.

'Must be broken,' said Kenningworth, putting it in his pocket.

The boys raced off to the bothy and Kenningworth hopped into the time machine.

'There's not a lot of room, is there?' he said. 'Where are you fellows going to sit?'

Mildew and Sponge looked at each other, then at Kenningworth, then back at each other. There was nothing for it. Despite Kenningworth's protestations, Mildew and Sponge sat down on his lap and, after making sure the calibrations were correct, Mildew pulled the lever. A flash and a whine and they had arrived.

'Are you sure we are back at the right time?' said Kenningworth, tipping the boys from his lap.

'Positive,' said Mildew. 'I suppose we'd better find the others. They still don't know what occurred on Pug's Peak with the teachers.'

'Of course,' said Sponge.

They headed for the door, but as they reached it, Kenningworth stopped and hung his head.

'Come on,' said Mildew. 'No time to lose.'

'I heard you, you know,' said Kenningworth without turning round.

'Heard us what?' said Mildew.

'I heard you say that you'd thought I'd left you behind,' said Kenningworth.

'Oh,' said Mildew. 'Well, we didn't know what to think.'

'Apart from the worst of me,' said Kenningworth.

'Sorry, Kenningworth,' said Mildew. 'We were wrong.'

'To be fair though you are a bit of a blot,' said Sponge.

'Yes,' said Kenningworth, heading out of the door. 'I suppose I am.'

Kenningworth suddenly froze. Mildew and Sponge could see why when they stepped forward and looked over his shoulder. There was a familiar white-haired figure standing just outside the bothy.

'Mr Particle,' said Mildew, stepping in front of the startled Kenningworth.

So it was Mr Particle who was responsible for the time machine being in the bothy when Mildew, Sponge and Kenningworth found it before their trip to the future.

'Ah,' he replied a little sheepishly. 'Mildew … Sponge … Kenningworth. What brings you to the bothy?'

Kenningworth peered at the physics teacher in fearful astonishment.

'But you're dead …'

Mildew quickly slapped his hand over Kenningworth's mouth.

'You're dedicated,' said Sponge. '*Ded*-icated.'

'I hope so,' said Mr Particle with a smile.

'We were just having a discussion about who among the teachers was the most dedicated and Kenningworth said it was definitely you.'

Mr Particle blushed.

'That's very kind of you, Kenningworth,' said Mr Particle. 'I had no idea you held me in such high esteem. You always give every impression of being bored to distraction in my lessons. Remember when I had to wake you up that time with the Bunsen burner?'

'Yes, sir,' said Kenningworth.

Before Mildew could stop him he leaned forward and prodded Mr Particle in the chest.

'You're solid,' he said. 'Or at least you seem solid. But are you?'

'These are all good talking points for the next

physics lesson,' said Mr Particle with a chuckle.

'Where have you been, sir?' said Mildew.

'Been?' said Mr Particle. 'I … I … Well, I have just actually been into the school but I appear to have slightly misjudged the settings – the settings on my … on my watch. The staff room is empty and there were what appeared to be girls wandering about. I think I need to get back to the time … to work. I need to get back to work. Run along now.'

Mr Particle disappeared inside the bothy and slammed the door behind him. Within moments there was a flash and whine and when they opened the door again, Mr Particle and the time machine were gone. Kenningworth stared in amazement.

'Look out!' said Sponge.

Kevin the giant floating eyeball was heading towards the bothy across the sports field.

# Eyeballing the Bothy

The boys scampered off to a convenient piece of shrubbery and peeked out through the twigs as Kevin came floating eerily over the sports field. The eyeball hovered outside the bothy, trying to peer in through the filthy windows, and then moved over to float like a balloon outside the door.

'It must have seen the flash of the time machine,' whispered Mildew.

The boys gasped as there was another flash and familiar whine from inside the bothy. Kevin seemed to become agitated and trembled violently.

'What on earth?' said Kenningworth.

'Who's this?' whispered Sponge. 'Is Particle coming back?'

'I rather think,' said Mildew with a sigh, 'that it may be us.'

Sure enough, another Mildew swung open the door and then, just as quickly, slammed it shut. Kenningworth could scarcely believe his eyes. Seeing his deceased physics teacher was one thing, but seeing a second Mildew was almost too much for his brain to cope with.

Another flash and whine followed and the other Mildew and Sponge had returned to the past. Kevin the giant floating eyeball drifted off again and the boys felt able to come out from their hiding place.

'The aliens will have seen everything,' said Mildew. 'They saw inside the bothy when I opened the door. They have seen the time machine.'

'Thank goodness we sent it back again!' said Sponge.

'Indeed,' said Mildew. 'Imagine what these monsters might achieve if they possessed a time machine. We can't let them have it.'

'But what if it comes back?' said Sponge. 'The

time machine, I mean. What if Mr Particle has made dozens of little trips like this one? The poor man still doesn't know he's dead.'

Mildew frowned.

'And then there's the werewolfery,' said Mildew.

'Werewolfery? Are you trying to say old Particle is the werewolf?' said Kenningworth.

'A bit, yes,' said Mildew. 'Was. He's not one now. Because he's dead. Although I suppose he might be one in the future.'

'You mustn't tell anyone, Kenningworth,' said Sponge. 'It's a secret. The time machine. No one knows except us and Mr Luckless. Although the Headmaster knows about Mr Particle. And Flintlock. He shot him.'

'Shot him? Who?'

'Flintlock. He shot Mr Particle. Or the werewolf he had become.'

'I thought he died of a sudden illness,' said Kenningworth.

'Incredibly sudden, yes,' said Mildew.

'And you say old Luckless is in on the time machine?' said Kenningworth. 'How does he know?'

'He was great chums with Particle,' said Sponge. 'He had a bit of a visit to Roman times because he fell in love with –'

'Miss Livia!' said Kenningworth. 'Good Lord. He

brought a Roman back with him. And that bust. The one that looks like Sponge! Good grief, it *is* Sponge, isn't it? It's all starting to make sense. A bit …'

'But as Sponge says,' said Mildew, 'you can't breathe a word of it. You have to promise.'

'But you can't keep all this a secret any longer, you chumps. Those monsters will be after that time machine. We are in imminent danger of being vaporised. We need to find those alien criminals and quickly. Normally I'm all for sneakery and fibbing, but in this case I don't see we have any choice – we have to tell the others.'

'Kenningworth does – unusually – have a point,' said Sponge.

Mildew nodded.

'Agreed, old friend,' said Mildew. 'Agreed.'

'Not that it's going to help much,' said Kenningworth. 'We don't have the time machine and we don't have these renegade aliens they are so keen on. All we have is those girls. We could give them those, though I hardly think they'd –'

'That's it!' cried Mildew.

'What's what?' said Kenningworth.

'Come on!' cried Mildew, setting off towards the school.

# 20 Girls from Another World

Enderpenny, Hipflask, Filbert and Furthermore, along with every other boy at Maudlin Towers, were waiting for them in the hall when Kenningworth, Mildew and Sponge returned to the school – only a short time after they had left as far as the other boys were concerned.

'How did it go?' said Enderpenny. 'Where are the teachers?'

'Up on Pug's Peak, dangling four feet off the ground,' said Sponge. 'The aliens have them.'

There were gasps from the assembled boys.

'What?' said Enderpenny.

'It's true,' said Mildew. 'The Neenor have them in their grip and still want these criminal aliens they keep going on about.'

'Speaking of aliens,' said Kenningworth, 'just to

make sure we get on with it, the Neenor sent this to keep an eye on us …'

Kevin the giant floating eyeball bobbed up and down outside the window.

'Aaaaargh!' cried the boys.

'You've already seen it, Sponge,' said Mildew.

'I know,' said Sponge. 'But it hasn't helped.'

'What is it?' said Hipflask.

'It's a giant floating eyeball,' said Sponge.

'We can see that,' said Hipflask. 'Why is it looking at us and where did it come from?'

'It's some kind of spy for the Neenor up on Pug's Peak. Everything it sees, they see.'

'Wait a minute,' said Furthermore. 'Didn't you suggest that the aliens might be giant floating eyeballs?'

'Mildew has quite a lot to tell you,' said Kenningworth. 'About a certain time machine …'

'A time machine?' said Furthermore.

'We haven't got time for that now!' said Mildew. 'I've cracked it!'

'What?' said Kenningworth.

'The girls!' cried Mildew. 'They are the aliens the other aliens are after!'

The boys stared at him in amazement.

'You know, I think he may be right,' said Furthermore. 'Again.'

'Nonsense,' said Kenningworth. 'I've seen girls on several occasions and they were almost exactly the same as these specimens.'

'Kenningworth is right,' said Footstool. 'I have a sister and she looks very similar.'

These testimonials seemed very compelling.

'Think about it,' said Mildew. 'Who else has arrived at Maudlin Towers recently? We were fools not to see it sooner. Let's find out what they have to say about it. But we must proceed with caution …'

'Agreed,' said Kenningworth. 'You two go and nose about. We'll watch from a safe distance.'

'That wasn't exactly what I … Oh, never mind. Come on, Sponge.'

Mildew and Sponge found the girls gathered together in the cloisters. The sight of so many of them almost made them lose courage and bolt for it, but they soldiered on. The girlish chatter ended as soon as the boys came within earshot. Milk and Spoon came forward warily.

'Greetings,' said Mildew with all the confidence he could muster. 'My name is Arthur Mildew. Of the Berkshire Mildews. You may remember us from our earlier conversations. My friend Master Spongely-Partwork and I wondered if we might join you.'

'Join us?' said Spoon with a frown. 'Why? Why would you join forces with us?'

'Not join forces exactly,' said Mildew.

'Quiet, Spoon,' said Milk. 'He just means they want to sit with us.'

'Oh,' said Spoon. 'Why didn't he say that?'

'Of course,' said Milk with a quick glance at her friend. 'Please be seated. But what happened to your teachers? Miss MT2T has not returned either.'

'I think it's better if we sit down,' said Mildew.

Milk and Spoon sat on the low wall and Mildew and Sponge stood next to them. The other girls backed off and talked among themselves. A long pause ensued.

Clouds rolled by above. Mildew noticed a cobweb in the floral moulding of a nearby column and Sponge developed a fascination with his thumb.

'The weather is quite similar to the weather of

earlier in the day,' said Milk eventually.

'Almost identical,' agreed Mildew. 'But that's Maudlin Towers for you.'

'Although the breeze is a little more damp,' said Sponge.

'That is true,' said Spoon. 'I noticed that.'

There was another long pause in conversation.

'I wonder if the weather tomorrow will be as similar to today's as today's weather was as similar to the weather of yesterday?' said Milk.

'Are you creatures from another world?' asked Mildew.

'Creatures from another world?' said Spoon with a splutter. 'Of course not. Why ever would you imagine such a thing? Creatures from another world? Creatures from another world? We are just girls. Ordinary human-type girls of the girlish kind. Creatures from another world – ha, the very idea!'

She laughed like a giddy woodpecker.

'Steady,' said Milk.

'It's no good! He's dragged it out of me. Yes! Yes! We are the aliens you seek.'

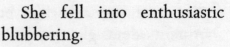

She fell into enthusiastic blubbering.

'Ha!' said Mildew. 'I knew it!'

'Oh, well done,' said Sponge.

'Stop crying, Spoon,' said Milk. 'Be brave.'

Spoon managed to control herself. The rest of the alien girls came to stand alongside them and Kenningworth and the other boys joined Mildew and Sponge. Both sides eyed each other warily.

'So it seems you have to hand yourself in to these Neenor creatures,' said Kenningworth.

'No!' cried Milk.

'But if you don't they are going to vaporise us. And I have the distinct impression that it will be rather unpleasant.'

Spoon collapsed into sobs again and Milk comforted her, turning to face the boys.

'We are innocent,' she cried. 'You have to believe us. They are merciless monsters.'

'We know!' said Hipflask. 'That's the point.'

'Why can't you simply escape?' said Mildew. 'Why not sneak back to your space-carriage and fly away?'

'We have run out of fuel,' said Milk.

'This is all well and good, but the fact is those monsters are going to frazzle our planet unless we hand you over,' said Enderpenny. 'What did you do anyway? Why are those horrors after you? What have you done?'

'It's a long story,' said Milk.

'All the same,' said Mildew, 'we probably ought to hear it.'

# 21 Whiznixoflax

The boys of Maudlin Towers quietened down expectantly and the girls did likewise, and Milk and Spoon took their places in front of them. They paused to gather their thoughts, then began.

'We are sorry to have brought such danger to your planet,' said Milk. 'It was not our intention.'

'What was your intention, exactly?' said Furthermore. 'Why come to Earth at all? And why this particularly dreary part of it?'

'We were escaping the Neenor,' said Milk. 'Trying to

get home. But we ran out of fuel.'

'And just happened to land on the very same planet the Neenor landed on millions of years ago?' said Furthermore.

'I know,' said Milk. 'What are the chances? It's like one of those amazing coincidences you get in books.'

'Amazing coincidences?' said Kenningworth.

'Oh yes,' said Mildew. 'Books are stuffed with them. You don't read enough fiction, that's your trouble, Kenningworth.'

'Go on,' said Sponge.

'We scanned for signs of fuel and it brought us here,' said Spoon.

'What fuel?' said Kenningworth. 'There's barely enough coal in the scuttles of Maudlin Towers to heat this place as it is. If you take that, we'll freeze. I can barely –'

'Coal?' said Milk. 'We have no need of your coal. The craft we came in uses whiznixoflax and nothing else.'

'Whiznixowhat?' said Furthermore. 'We have nothing like that here.'

The two girls whispered together.

'We think you may call whiznixoflax by the Earth name "jewels",' said Milk.

'Jewels?' said Furthermore. 'Your vessel runs on jewels?'

The girls nodded.

'That sounds expensive,' said Sponge.

'On the contrary,' said Milk. 'One piece of whiznixoflax can power a craft for thousands of years and for millions of miles. Not only that, it powers our ability to breathe your atmosphere and to block the scanners of the Neenor.'

'But you look just like us,' said Furthermore. 'I would have imagined there might be a greater diversity of life in the universe. How strange that your race should also evolve into a humanoid form.'

'Oh – we look nothing like you,' said Spoon. 'We have the ability to make you think this is what we look like. We are able to affect those parts of your brain concerned with perception and give you this illusion. It is quite harmless, rest assured.'

'So what do you actually look like?' said Kenningworth. 'Are you green? I saw some aliens in a book once and they were green. Lime green with little antennae.'

'Not all aliens are green,' said Spoon. 'It's not as though we are Riglosians!'

This was greeted by enthusiastic chuckling from all of the alien girls.

'It is perhaps better that you do not know what we actually look like,' said Milk, her expression serious once more.

'So if you found some whiznixoflax, you'd be able to escape,' said Sponge.

'We might,' said Spoon.

'Our readings show that you have quite a store of jewels here at Maudlin Towers,' said Milk.

'We do?' said Enderpenny.

'Yes. And among them is indeed the whiznixoflax we are hunting for. But we've searched the school and found nothing. The readings are strongest next to that badly repaired bust of you, Sponge. If we can get the jewels to our podule there may still be a chance we can escape the Neenor.'

Mildew and Sponge looked at each other.

'Oh dear,' said Mildew. 'I'm afraid we did have a hoard of jewels. They were indeed stored in Sponge's bust. But they were stolen. We don't have them any more. Sorry.'

Milk groaned and Spoon's eyes filled with tears.

'Our scanner must have picked up a record of them,' said Milk. 'Right place, wrong time.'

'Shame we haven't got the time machine, Mildew,' said Kenningworth. 'We could pop back and fetch them.'

'A time machine?' said Milk, wide-eyed. 'You have a time machine?'

Mildew sighed.

'I suppose we may as well tell them, Sponge.'

'You're right,' he replied.

So Mildew and Sponge told everyone assembled all about the time machine that Mr Particle had invented, about the part it played in their returning of the School Spoon, their journey to the Viking age, Sponge's journey to Roman times, Mr Luckless and his love of the Roman Miss Livia, Lord Marzipan Maudlin, and Mr Particle's death at the hands of Flintlock while in his werewolf form.

Not even Kenningworth interrupted this tale, so agog were all the listeners, human and alien.

'Oh – and Sponge and I popped into the future a couple of times. Into the distant future when people talk to themselves holding small flat oblongs to their heads and where biscuits are astonishingly expensive ...'

'I went there too!' said Kenningworth excitedly.

'And once just a little into the future,' said Sponge. 'To a point that is now very slightly in the past. That's where we saw Kevin the giant floating eyeball.'

'But this is wonderful,' said Milk. 'We can use the time machine to escape!'

'Except we don't have the time machine any more,' said Mildew.

'Why not?' said Milk.

'It's gone back into the past,' said Sponge. 'It may

come back if someone from the past has gone into the future. The future for them, that is.'

This explanation seemed to exhaust Sponge's brain and he staggered sideways dizzily.

'So all is lost?' said Milk tearfully.

'Never give up hope,' said Mildew. 'Sponge and I have been in all manner of scrapes where we thought we were about to be squished but we've always managed to pull through.'

'Mildew's right,' said Sponge. 'Things have a way of sorting themselves out.'

'I hope you're right,' said Milk. 'I really do. But it seems utterly hopeless right now.'

# Greenbeard

The boys and alien girls had fallen silent for a while, rather weighed down by the enormity of their current predicament. No light was appearing at the end of the very long and dark tunnel in which they now sat.

As if to further darken it, Zigg and Tarduz had wandered down the hill and passed by the window, their metal legs clanking and squeaking. They appeared to have worn themselves out in the effort and stood for a moment, wheezing.

'What are they doing?' said Sponge.

'Who knows,' said Mildew.

'We have less than an hour left!' cried Enderpenny.

There was a collective gasp.

'But I don't understand,' said Furthermore. 'If your vessel uses jewels as a fuel, why don't you search elsewhere? There are jewels all over this planet. There are jewellers' shops full of them. There are mines. There are –'

'And how would they get there?' said Kenningworth. 'They are trapped here!'

'No – not any jewels, in any case,' said Milk. 'Whiznixoflax are incredibly rare and powerful. Only one has ever been recorded in this sector of the galaxy. We have a special scanner that picks up its trace and shows its history. We know where it has been for centuries. Look …'

Milk took out a small device from her pocket, tapped it a few times and it projected an image of a large ball on to the wall.

'What is that?' said Mildew.

'Don't you recognise your own planet?' said Spoon.

The boys gasped.

'From our records the whiznixoflax came to Earth via a meteor shower many thousands of years ago. A portion of the meteor was found by a goatherd in a place you call China.

'It was kept in his family as a treasured item

until sold to a trader by his widow many years after his death. From there it travelled along the Silk Road and on to Constantinople and then to Venice, where it was broken by accident to reveal the whiznixoflax within. Believing it to be an ordinary, if precious, jewel, it was made into a ring for a sister of the Doge of Venice.

'Centuries later the descendants of that lady, much reduced in circumstances and wealth, decided to emigrate to America, taking the ring with them. The ship was bound for Boston when it was intercepted by a vessel under the command of a jewel-obsessed pirate captain called –'

'Greenbeard?' cried Mildew and Sponge.

'You've heard of him?'

'Mildew is an ancestor,' said Sponge.

'Descendant,' said Mildew.

'I always get that wrong,' said Sponge.

'Greenbeard is your ancestor?' said Milk excitedly. 'Then do you have the whiznixoflax? Might he have handed it down to you?'

Mildew sighed.

'No,' he said. 'If it was here, then it would have been among all the other jewels that were snaffled.'

'So where are they now?' said Milk.

'No one knows,' said Sponge. 'They could be anywhere.'

'But the scanner is still showing them as being somewhere close by,' said Milk, tapping the device. 'Although it seems not to be working properly. It says they are here and yet it also says they are not. Very confusing.'

'They were last seen heading west in a balloon,' said Mildew. 'Your machine must be faulty.'

'Even so,' said Milk. 'I have to keep trying. If we can find the whiznixoflax we can at least draw the Neenor away from this planet. I'm going to carry on scanning.'

With that she walked away.

'Who are you, anyway?' said Kenningworth. 'You never told us.'

'We are children, just like you,' said Spoon. 'But we were taken from our parents by the Neenor and forced to live in a terrible place, far away. It's on the dark side of a damp moon and is perpetually gloomy.

'It is a frightening and fearful place where we are forced to perform boring and pointless tasks over and over again. It's probably hard for you to understand.'

'I don't know,' said Kenningworth. 'It has a familiar ring to it.'

'But why did your parents let them take you?' said Sponge.

'They had no choice,' said Spoon. 'The Neenor kidnapped us in order to make our parents do their bidding. Our families are slaves of these monsters, kept in line by the fear of what will happen to their children. When we are old enough we will in turn become slaves.'

'That's horrible,' said Sponge.

'Yes,' said Spoon. 'We chose to escape because some of us were about to be vaporised for crimes against the Mordentor Federation. We had nothing to lose. We stole a podule and this is as far as we got.'

'What was your crime?' said Mildew.

'Oh,' said Spoon. 'Among the many pointless tasks we were given, we were asked to write a long essay about how the Great One had improved the lives of so many living on planets in the Mordentor Federation, but someone …'

Here she cast a quick glance in the direction in which Milk had gone.

'Milk forgot to pass on the note telling the rest of

us that it had to be in by the following moonrise. She feels very bad about it.'

'Wait,' said Mildew. 'Are you saying that the hideous crime the Neenor accused you of, the one they thought so terrible they could hardly mention – one that meant they chased you across the universe and threatened to vaporise our planet unless we handed you over – was basically that you hadn't done your homework?'

Spoon shrugged.

'The monsters,' said Kenningworth. 'Even old Drumlin isn't that strict.'

'Who are the Neenor anyway?' said Furthermore.

'They weren't always like this,' said Spoon. 'The Neenor were a peaceful race until a party of their explorers searching the universe in the service of the advancement of knowledge arrived at a far-flung planet and found a creature there.'

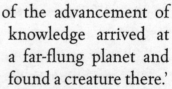

'Mr Stupendo,' said Mildew.

'The Neenor brought this human home with the intention of studying him, but the creature quickly became dominant

164

and they became subject to his iron will.

'He turned them from a race of happy, peaceful academics into furiously competitive tyrants. Competitive sport became a religion to them.'

'What happened to the Great One?'

'The Great One died many millennia ago, but before he did the Neenor used their advanced technology to turn him into a kind of self-aware hologram.'

'A hologram?'

'It's like a projection of something – it has no form except as an image. You might think of it as a ghost.'

'Stupendo is a ghost?' said Mildew, horrified.

'In a way,' said Spoon.

'The hologram now rules in his stead and his cruel regime is enforced as a religion by the fanatical Neenor.'

The boys groaned.

'Maudlin Towers has exported its misery to the galaxy,' cried Mildew. 'Sports teachers should never be allowed power. Everyone knows that!'

'So you know the Great One?' said Spoon.

'Oh yes,' said Mildew. 'We most certainly do.'

'This is all our fault,' said Sponge. 'Because it was we who sent the Great One back in time to be taken by the Neenor in the first place.'

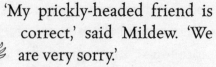

'My prickly-headed friend is correct,' said Mildew. 'We are very sorry.'

'Oh no,' said Furthermore. 'Mordentor. It's Maudlin Towers, isn't it? Mordentor. Maudlin Towers. The words have been sanded down a bit by the passage of time.'

'We're to blame!' shouted Mildew.

'You could never have known,' said Spoon.

'Odd that you tracked the jewels to Maudlin Towers though,' said Furthermore. 'You would have thought it might have tracked them to wherever they are now.'

'True,' said Spoon. 'That is odd. It's almost as though they were still here. But they can't be. Oh, what are we going to do?'

None of the boys had a satisfactory answer to this, and with a long sigh, Spoon walked away.

'What are we going to do, Mildew?' asked Sponge when she was out of earshot.

'I don't know, old friend,' he replied. 'I really don't know. And our time is running out …'

# 23 A Black-clad Girl From the Future

**M**ilk did not return and Zigg and Tarduz were now standing in the sports field drumming their legs impatiently on the grass. Mildew and Sponge watched them through the window.

Spoon gathered her fellow alien girls together and much whispering ensued. After a few moments they approached the boys, their faces cast down, their expressions a picture of despair and desolation.

'We have talked among ourselves,' said Spoon, 'and we have agreed that we will give ourselves up. We should have done it before. We can't allow your planet to suffer on our account.'

'No,' said Mildew. 'We can't let you surrender to those monsters.'

'Thank you,' said Spoon. 'But we have placed you all in danger and it is time for us to leave you in peace.'

'No!' said Kenningworth forcefully.

The boys turned to him in surprise.

'I've had my fill of being bossed around by those eight-legged abominations,' he said. 'I may seem like a bit of a blot sometimes …' He looked at Mildew and Sponge. 'Maybe I *am* a bit of a blot sometimes. But there comes a time when one has to say: enough is enough.

'If we get vaporised, then so be it. At least I won't have to go to my cousin Rupert's wedding a week next Thursday. Or wear the ghastly velvet suit my mother has had made for me.'

'Kenningworth is right,' said Mildew. 'You can't do it. We're all in this together. We all agree, don't we, boys?'

The other boys nodded their assent.

'But what are we going to do?' said Filbert. 'Are we just going to wait to be vaporised?'

'I don't really want to be vaporised,' said Sponge.

'At least there won't be any soup,' said Mildew.

'Soup?' said Spoon.

'It's what we say instead of blood,' said Mildew. 'Because …'

Sponge teetered sideways and was caught by Mildew.

'Ah,' said Spoon. 'I'm not very keen on soup myself.'

Sponge smiled weakly in his wibbliness.

'But we won't let you just give into these horrors,' said Sponge, straightening himself up. 'It's not right.'

'The Neenor are behaving more and more oddly,' said Mildew, peering out of the window as Zigg tried to give the passing Kevin a flick with one of its feet but missed and fell over, sending Tarduz sprawling too. 'They'll probably vaporise us anyway just for the fun of it.'

'They are acting strangely, aren't they?' said Sponge. 'I've noticed that. They seemed just odd in an alien-type way before, but now they seem more … more … I can't quite put my finger on it.'

'Yes,' said Kenningworth. 'You're right. They

are getting odder. No – not odder, exactly. More stupid.'

'I have a theory about that,' said Furthermore.

Kenningworth rolled his eyes.

'What is it?' said Spoon.

'I think the mind-connector must, to some degree, be two-way. So although the aliens can go into your minds and search about at will, there is also danger of contamination.'

Mildew and Sponge stared at Furthermore for a while, then at each other, and both shrugged in bafflement. Kenningworth chuckled.

'He's saying the aliens have become infected with your idiocy, you pair of dimwits.'

Furthermore nodded.

'Basically, yes, I am,' he said.

'How dare you?' said Sponge. 'That's outrageous.'

'Ah – hello, boys,' said Mr Painly, wandering towards them. 'And ladies. You haven't seen the rest of the staff, have you?'

'Mr Painly!' cried the boys.

'How did you escape, sir?' said Mildew.

'Escape what?' said Mr Painly.

'Didn't you hear the

Headmaster's announcement?'

'I hear nothing when I'm reading *The Bored Boy's Book of Moderately Diverting Things*. What's happening? Why are you all clustered together in this strange fashion?'

'We have been invaded by creatures from another world, sir,' said Mildew.

Mr Painly smiled and opened his mouth to speak.

'Not the girls, sir,' said Mildew. 'Although …'

'Real aliens, sir,' said Sponge. 'From another planet and such forth.'

'Nonsense,' said Mr Painly. 'Don't think you boys can fool me so easily.'

'Show him the drawing, Mildew,' said Furthermore.

Mildew reached into his pocket, took out the drawing and solemnly unfolded it in front of Mr Painly.

'Oh, sweet merciful heavens,' he said. 'It's true!'

Mildew recapped all of the previous events to the bemused Mr Painly, who sat scratching his head in wonder with every new revelation. He seemed particularly intrigued by the notion of the aliens being contaminated by Mildew and Sponge's simple-mindedness.

'So you say that the aliens are behaving more and

more like you and Master Spongely-Partwork?' he asked. 'Curious.'

'Some sort of cross-contamination from their mind probe,' said Furthermore.

'This gives me an idea!' said Mildew.

Kenningworth groaned.

'Hear him out,' said Mr Painly. 'We are desperate, after all.'

Mildew frowned.

'Thank you, sir. Well, if what Furthermore suggests is true, then I think we may be able to stop them.'

'But how?' cried Sponge.

Mildew smiled.

'Maths!' said Mildew.

'Maths?' said Sponge. 'But how can that cruel magic be used against the Neenor?'

Mildew tapped the side of his nose.

'Wait and see,' said Mildew. 'Mr Painly. A quick word, if you please.'

'Hello,' came a now familiar voice behind them.

They all turned to see the black-clad girl from the future walking towards them. The boys and girls stared at her in amazement. Enderpenny was about to point out her black nail varnish when Mildew spoke.

'I was wondering when you'd appear,' he said.

'You don't seem very surprised to see me,' she said. 'Or very cross that I took your time machine.'

'We already know,' said Sponge.

'Who is this?' said Furthermore. 'Is she another alien?'

'She's from the future,' said Mildew. 'Sorry, you never did tell us your name.'

'Oh. It's Ella. What's yours?'

'Mildew,' he replied. 'And this is Sponge.'

Ella peered at the girls.

'I thought this was a boys-only school back in your day,' she said. 'What are they doing here?'

'It is,' said Mildew. 'These girls only look like girls. In reality they are creatures from another world. Our teachers are held captive up on that hill by giant mechanical spiders whilst that giant floating eyeball spies on us …'

Kevin drifted by the window.

'Cool,' said Ella.

'I've just thought of a plan to destroy those monsters and stop them from vaporising the planet,' said Mildew. 'So you need to go to the time machine and take it back to us in the future where you left us stranded, so we can return here where I come up with this idea. Do you see?'

'I ... think ... so ...' said Ella.

'Good,' said Mildew. 'Thank you. When you get to the future you'll find us standing looking baffled in front of the talking painting in the school hall.'

'I'd rather stay here,' she said with a weak smile.

'But you can't,' said Mildew. 'Sorry. In any case, you will only get vaporised along with us if you do.'

The girl nodded and began to walk away, before coming back and hurriedly kissing Mildew on the cheek. Then she headed off to the bothy.

'What a strange person,' said Mildew, frowning and blushing and breaking out into a sweat.

'You look faint, Mildew,' said Sponge.

'What?' said Mildew, leaning on a chair for support.

'Mildew!' said Sponge. 'Pull yourself together!'

Mildew shook his head and stared off to the door through which Ella had recently departed.

'Wait!' shouted Mildew. 'Ella!'

'Really, Mildew,' said Sponge. 'There are more important things to –'

'Shhh, Sponge,' said Mildew. 'She's got the time machine!'

'I know!' said Sponge. 'But –'

'Come on. I'll explain on the way!'

# Felicity Fallowfield (again)

*E*lla was just entering the bothy as Mildew and Sponge galumphed up behind her, gasping for breath. Mildew had tried to explain to Sponge on the way, but all he had managed was 'past', 'bust' and 'jewels'.

'Ella, wait!' said Mildew.

She turned round.

'What is it?' she said.

'Change of plan,' said Mildew. 'We need the time machine.'

'But what about rescuing yourselves from the future?' she asked.

'That will have to wait,' he replied.

'Will you please tell me what's going on?' said Sponge, only just getting his breath back.

Mildew took a deep breath and explained.

'The alien girls need the whiznixoflax to power their craft and the whiznixoflax was in Greenbeard's hoard of jewels …'

'Which was stolen by Felicity Fallowfield,' said Sponge.

'Wait – who's this Felicity Fallowfield character and what's all this about a hoard of jewels?' said Ella.

'Greenbeard was a pirate,' said Mildew. 'He had a thing about jewels. Couldn't get enough of them. He stashed them away in Maudlin Towers, where they were subsequently stolen by one Felicity Fallowfield, international girl of mystery and serial jewel-thief. One of those jewels is apparently something called whiznixoflax and it is fuel for the alien craft. So I thought we could –'

'Go back to before the theft and rescue the jewels,' said Sponge.

'Well … yes,' said Mildew. 'Exactly.'

'That's very clever,' said Ella.

Mildew blushed.

'But wait – the jewels were stolen,' said Sponge. 'We saw them get stolen.'

'We have to try, old fig,' said Mildew.

'Let's go, then,' said Ella.

'No … That is … the time machine … There just isn't the room really …'

'Rubbish,' said Ella. 'We'll just have to scrunch up a bit.'

'I don't like the sound of that,' said Sponge.

'Well, I don't see why I should miss out on the fun,' said Ella.

Ella proved impervious to all objections put forward by the boys and so they did indeed scrunch up a bit. Dials were arranged and the lever pulled and with the usual flatulent whine, they hurtled back in time.

They crept out of the bothy and along the ha-ha, taking great care not to be seen by anyone – including themselves.

'If my calculations are correct …' said Mildew as they crept down the path running alongside the school, 'and I think they are … then we should have arrived back just as …'

There was a sudden crash from inside the entrance hall.

'There goes Sponge's bust!' said Mildew. 'Quickly!'

Mildew hurried off across the lawn towards the kitchen garden.

'Where are you going?' hissed Sponge. 'The jewels are this way!'

'Not for long,' said Mildew over his shoulder. 'Come on!'

Sponge and Ella set off after Mildew and they all bolted through the door in the high garden wall that led to a courtyard and the old coach house with its little clock on the roof.

'It's almost time,' said Mildew as they ran across the gravel and stood together outside a small side door.

'What are we doing?' whispered Ella.

'Yes,' said Sponge. 'What *are* we doing, exactly?'

Mildew did not reply but placed a finger to his lips to signal to them to be quiet and then opened the door.

'Whoah!' whispered Ella.

They found themselves in a vast dark space – much larger than it had seemed from the outside – containing something huge and strange, difficult, at first, to make out in the gloom.

'Of course!' said Sponge. 'Felicity's escape balloon!'

'I felt sure this must be where she had hidden it,' said Mildew. 'It seemed the only place large enough.'

'Well done,' said Sponge.

'So this Felicity person makes off in this balloon?' said Ella. 'With the jewels?'

'Yes,' said Sponge. 'It was very annoying.'

'But how are you going to get the jewels?' said Ella.

Ella and Sponge looked at Mildew expectantly.

'I don't know,' said Mildew. 'I can't be expected to think of everything.'

Sponge groaned.

'It's hopeless,' he said. 'We know she escapes. We saw her do it. This just means we are going to see her escape again. And it was annoying enough last time.'

They waited in silence and sure enough they heard hurried footsteps.

'Shhh,' said Mildew. 'She's coming.'

They just managed to duck out of sight as one of the huge doors was dragged open and Felicity Fallowfield came in, the bag of jewels in her hand. She walked towards the basket of the hot-air balloon, put the bag down next to it and went back to open the other door. The door seemed to stick and Felicity struggled to move it.

'Quickly,' whispered Mildew. 'Find something we can swap for the jewels.'

Sponge peered about in the gloom and saw a small coal scuttle filled with coal.

Ella followed his gaze and they both went over to gather some pieces of coal and scurry back. Mildew and Sponge decanted the jewels into their pockets and then replaced them with the coal.

'She's coming back,' hissed Mildew. 'Hide.'

Felicity Fallowfield strode back, picked up the bag of what she assumed were still jewels and tossed them into the basket, pausing to wonder at the small squeak that seemed to come from inside.

She dragged the basket out of the coach house, and with the agility for which she was famed, leaped into the basket with a single bound. Within seconds, she had struck a match, lit the flame and was rising up into the air, where a southerly breeze bore her away towards Pug's Peak.

'We did it,' said Mildew as he walked towards the open doorway, his pockets full of jewels.

'Cool,' said Ella.

'All we need to do now is head back to the time machine and … wait a minute. Where's Sponge?'

'I haven't see him since we hid from Felicity,' said Ella.

'Sponge!' called Mildew, stepping

back inside the coach house. 'Sponge! Where are you?'

'There's nowhere left for him to hide,' said Ella. 'It's like he's disappeared.'

'Oh no,' said Mildew.

'What?' said Ella.

'Oh, Sponge,' he said, shaking his head.

'You don't mean … ?'

Mildew nodded.

'He must have hidden in the basket of the balloon!'

# Sponge in a Balloon

'So long, boys! Maybe we'll meet again one day!' cried Felicity Fallowfield, waving as she floated away from Maudlin Towers in her hot-air balloon.

'It's getting chilly,' she said, before reaching down to grab a cloak she'd stashed away in the basket for just this eventuality. As she lifted it up, she found Sponge curled up beneath it, revealed now like a tortoise without its shell.

'What on earth?' said Felicity. 'But I … You were down there … I just saw you …'

'I know,' said Sponge. 'It's very complicated.'

'What are you doing in here?' said Felicity. 'If you have come to try and stop me I should warn you that may not end well for you.'

Sponge gulped.

Felicity looked down at the bag of jewels and then at Sponge, before smiling and picking it up.

'I admire your pluck, Sponge,' she said. 'But I'm afraid I'm going to have to ask you to leave.'

'Leave?' said Sponge. 'But we're up in the air. A long way up in the air. I don't like heights!'

'You should have thought about that before you got in,' replied Felicity. 'You're weighing down my balloon. Besides, you won't be high up for very long.'

Felicity grinned. Sponge folded his arms.

'I won't and you can't make me,' he said.

Felicity grinned, laced her fingers together and cracked her knuckles.

'Oh, can't I?' she said.

Sponge whimpered.

Just then, the basket of the balloon, which was indeed flying a little low due to the extra weight, struck one of the crags of Pig's Pike and tipped forward as it was dragged past. Felicity grabbed hold of the rim, but Sponge was hurled overboard, emitting a high-pitched squeal as he fell. He just managed to catch hold of a rope hanging down from the basket and was left swinging on the end of it like a fish on a line. His flailing about made the balloon jerk from side to side and lose height.

'Aaaargh!' cried Sponge, staring down at the boulder-strewn expanse between Pig's Pike and Pug's Peak. 'Help!'

Felicity Fallowfield leaned over the basket, stretching out her hand towards his.

'Come on, Sponge!' she said. 'Grab my hand!'

'I can't!' he said. 'If I let go I'll fall.'

'If you don't grab my hand you'll fall anyway!' she cried. 'Trust me. I'm sorry. I won't let you fall, I promise.'

'I can't!' he shouted.

'You can!' she replied.

'I can't!'

And with that plaintive cry, Sponge let go and fell. But due to the fact that the balloon had now arrived at the summit of Pug's Peak, the fall was only a matter of a couple of feet and Sponge plopped into a surprisingly soft patch of moss.

'Better luck next time, Sponge!' cried Felicity.

Sponge got to his feet, watching the balloon sail away, and allowed himself a smile, patting his jewel-filled pockets and wondering when Felicity would discover that her haul was really a bag of coal.

Sponge's smile did not last long though as he realised he was at the top of Pug's Peak and would have to get down.

He was sweating and gasping by the time he reached the bottom, and decided that the only thing he could do was head for the time machine in the hope that Mildew and Ella had not left without him.

Sponge was close to tears as he opened the door of the bothy, dreading to find it empty.

'Sponge!' cried Mildew, rushing forward to greet his friend. 'Thank goodness!'

'We were really worried,' said Ella.

Sponge blushed.

'And you still have the jewels?' said Mildew.

Sponge patted his pockets and smiled.

'Well done, old sock,' said Mildew.

'Do you think we have the whiznixoflax?' said Sponge.

'We can only hope so,' said Mildew.

In an instant they were back to Mildew and Sponge's own time.

'Quickly,' said Mildew as he disentangled himself from his fellow time travellers. 'Let's get the jewels to the girls!'

'Wait,' said Ella. 'I should really be getting back. Or forward. You know what I mean. My family are really boring but they'll still be missing me and I think we're having pizza tonight, so …'

Mildew and Sponge had no idea what 'pizza' might be or whether having it was a good or a bad thing, but they had to agree that Ella needed to go back to her own time. Otherwise they and Kenningworth would be stuck in future Maudlin Towers and none of this could happen.

Ella sat back down in the time machine and fiddled with the settings.

'I hope everything works out,' she said as Mildew stood back with Sponge.

'Thanks,' said Mildew.

'Yes, thanks,' said Sponge.

There followed an awkward pause – the kind where no one quite knows what to say but where everyone feels like they ought to be saying something.

'Bye, boys,' said Ella eventually, with a weak smile.

Then she pulled the lever, and just like that, she was gone.

Mildew and Sponge headed back to the hall and burst in through the doors after what, to those still in there, seemed only a short time since they had left in pursuit of Ella.

'Forget something?' said Kenningworth.

Mildew and Sponge grinned and marched forward to empty their pockets, tipping a cascade of sparkling jewels across the stage.

'But how … ?' said Enderpenny.

'Mildew was very clever,' said Sponge.

'Sponge was almost killed. Tell them, Sponge.'

'I was almost killed.'

Milk suddenly walked in.

'What's going on? I've given up. The scanner must be broken because it's led me all the way back –'

'The whiznixoflax!' cried Spoon. 'Look!'

Milk rushed over as Spoon lifted a pale pink, tear-shaped jewel from the collection.

'We can go home!' cried Milk, her eyes glistening with tears. 'But where did you find it?'

'It was Mildew and Sponge,' said Spoon.

'We travelled back in time to find Greenbeard's jewels,' said Mildew. 'It was nothing really.'

'Now we can escape and you will all be safe. Thank you. Thank you for all you have –'

'No!' said Mildew.

'What do you mean, "no"?' said Sponge. 'I don't want to be vaporised!'

'They'll vaporise us for letting them go!' said Mildew. 'Everyone knows you can't trust spiders. These monsters need dealing with and I still have a plan! Mr Painly, could I have that word now?'

Mildew and Sponge and Mr Painly gathered into a huddle. The boys and girls could not hear what they were saying but watched as, eventually, the three of them broke apart, smiling.

'I have to say, Mildew,' said Mr Painly, 'that is rather brilliant.'

'But will it work, sir?' said Sponge.

'Let's go and find out!' said Mildew.

# 26 (M)aths Saves (the) World

*L*ight was beginning to fade as Mildew and Sponge and Mr Painly headed off towards Pug's Peak. Some of their resolve started to fade too as they crossed the sports field.

'This may be our most discombobulating adventure yet, Sponge,' said Mildew.

'More discombobulating than werewolves or a giant floating eyeball?'

'Werewolves? Giant floating eyeballs?' said Mr Painly. 'How long was I reading that book?'

'It's all very complicated, sir,' said Sponge.

Mildew and Sponge turned to see Mr Painly in boggle-eyed panic induced by the sight of enormous mechanical spiders, who were clanking towards them.

'Where are the criminals?' boomed Zigg. 'And

where is the time machine? We have waited long enough!'

'And who is this?' yelled Tarduz.

Mr Painly shuffled forward.

'Painly,' he said tremulously.

'Where is our stuff?' they yelled.

'We won't tell you,' said Sponge.

'You will tell us now!' yelled Zigg, its voice a little more high-pitched than it had intended.

'Shan't,' said Mildew.

'Vaporise them!' cried Tarduz.

'We can't vaporise them, can we?' said Zigg. 'Because then we won't know anything. What about the time machine? Think what we could do with a time machine, old nebula.'

'I don't care any more. No – wait,' said Tarduz. 'We can use the mind-reading thingies.'

'Don't call them thingies. They're called … What are they called?'

'I can't remember,' said Tarduz. 'Doesn't matter. Thingy is fine.'

The thingies plopped on to Mildew and Sponge's heads and the aliens began to probe their minds.

'There's a lot of other stuff I can't remember lately,' continued Zigg.

'Yes – I haven't felt quite myself since we first connected with these Earthloids. You don't think there's a chance we have somehow been affected by their tiny brains?'

'I think you're right, old sun spot. Perhaps we should disconnect before its too –'

'Now, Mr Painly!' shouted Mildew.

'John is twelve but his sister Mary is Spanish. If Mary has thirty-two oranges and John has a haircut, how many baths will they have to fill by Wednesday if they are standing on the equator and facing due east?'

'What is he talking about?' said Zigg.

'I don't know, old probe,' said Tarduz. 'But these creatures are feeble in comparison to us. Our brains are mighty. Theirs are the size of piznakloids. Think! Think as hard as you can!'

'Again, Mr Painly!'

'A dog has three thousand and forty-two fleas but his master has two umbrellas. If the dog is called Jack and the umbrellas are all tartan, how long will it take Susan to get from Land's End to London if she travels three miles every alternate Wednesday?'

The legs of the spiders began to shudder and steam gushed from the joints as rivets started to ping this way and that, making the boys and Mr Painly dive for cover.

'A tree had five apples,' called Mr Painly from the bracken. 'One of them has twelve pips. Use this to ascertain how many windows the neighbouring house contains. Divide this figure by the number of Margarets in Hastings, calculating it to the nearest whole number and then express it as a type of fish – not including salmon or hake.'

All at once everything went quiet. Then there was a small pop from Zigg, and after a moment another from Tarduz. Both huge metal spiders swayed drunkenly before falling over with a great crash.

'It worked, Mildew,' said Sponge. 'But how?'

'I think, if our calculations are correct,' said Mildew, 'their brains went pop.'

'Urgh!' said Sponge. 'But also hurrah!'

'And given that they were pretty much all brain, that's the end of them, I reckon.'

Up on Pug's Peak, the teachers dropped back to earth, released from the grip of their alien captors, and hurried down the hillside. Mildew and Sponge and Mr Painly rushed towards the Headmaster and Mr Luckless to explain what had happened since they had been ensnared.

'But never fear,' said Mildew. 'We have defeated those murderous monsters and averted the imminent vaporisation of the planet. So not too bad.'

'Agreed, Mildew,' said the Headmaster. 'Mr Painly deserves our thanks.'

'Mr Painly, sir? But —'

'Shhh now, Mildew,' said the Headmaster. 'Don't steal Mr Painly's thunder.'

Mr Painly was raised up and carried shoulder high into the school with the staff cheering his name all the way.

'Of all the …' said Mildew.

'Come on, Mildew,' said Sponge with a comforting smile. 'We know it was us, don't we? That's the main thing.'

'Is it?' said Mildew.

'I don't know,' said Sponge. 'But let's say it is, shall we?'

Mildew nodded.

'All right then.'

27

Farewells

The staff and Mildew and Sponge returned to the hall, where the rest of the boys, Milk, Spoon and the alien girls waited anxiously to meet them. They were overjoyed to hear of the Neenor brain-popping that occurred on the sports field.

'That's wonderful,' said Spoon, hugging Sponge. 'You are so brave!'

Sponge blushed.

'Good work, you blisters,' said Kenningworth.

'Thanks, you blot,' said Sponge. 'It was Mildew, really.'

'You have saved the universe,' said Spoon.

'We have?' said Mildew.

'Yes. The Neenors are a hive mind, each one connected to the other. You will have set off a chain reaction through the entire race. Every Neenor brain will have gone pop. We are free!'

Spoon's words were almost entirely drowned out by the staff singing another round of 'For he's a jolly good fellow' to Mr Painly. Mildew sighed.

'So I gather the girls we are host to are not girls at all but aliens,' said the Headmaster as the staff finished their chorus and grouped around him to peer at the alien girls. 'I'm surprised you did not spot anything unusual, Miss MT2T.'

'We built Miss MT2T,' said Spoon.

'Built her?' said the Headmaster.

'From the waste disposal system in the podule,' said Spoon. 'We thought it might be more convincing if we had an adult with us. Sorry.'

The Headmaster peered at Miss MT2T.

'Sor … ry …' said Miss MT2T.

Night had now descended like a huge black sock and the girls explained that they really must be getting back to their ship.

'It is time for us to go,' said Milk. 'Thank you for all your help and for your kindness.'

'Oh … well … I …' burbled Mildew.

'Me too,' said Sponge.

'You are both very brave,' said Spoon.

'I'm really not,' said Sponge.

'But it's easy to be brave if you are courageous by

200

nature,' said Spoon. 'How much braver it is to show courage when your nature is timid.'

Both boys smiled.

'Must you go now?' said the Headmaster, looking disappointed. 'But I was hoping to take Miss MT2T on a tour of Lower Maudlin. It has very fine curb stones, you know.'

'Another … time,' said Miss MT2T. 'Thank you … for allowing us to survive. Your prisoners have … been very kind … to us.'

'Prisoners?' said the Headmaster. 'Oh, you mean the boys. Very droll.'

Mildew and Sponge glanced at each other.

'I'm afraid we really should be going,' said Milk. 'The XR7 interstellar highway is a nightmare if you catch it at peak time.'

'Thanks for having us,' said Spoon.

'It was our pleasure,' said Sponge.

'Well, maybe not "pleasure" exactly,' said Mildew. 'What with the mechanical spiders, the giant floating eyeballs, the threat of being vaporised and such forth.'

'True,' said Sponge. 'But all the same …'

'Might I ask what you are really called?' said Mildew. 'Milk and Spoon can't be your actual names. What would we call you were we ever to land on your planet?'

'Well,' said Milk. 'Actually, it's Figgle Ziggle Wiggle-Giggle Floo Floo Wizfig Wizbag Woo Woo Zipwire-Flujab Weeeeeeeeeeeeeeeeeeeeee Boing Ra Rar Zoom-Zoom Crisp Packet Toenail Lip Gloss Boo Hoo-Arrrrrr ggggggg hhhhhhhhhhhhhhhh Dum Dum-Dum Dum Dum Parp Wednesday Doo Dah Doo Dah-Plop Twang Marmalade Billingsgate Fishmarket.'

Mildew nodded.

'Shall we just continue to call you Milk for the time being?'

'Very well,' she said.

'What about you?' asked Sponge of Spoon.

Spoon let out a long, deep guttural belching sound that rattled the windows and the teeth in Sponge's head and echoed round the corridors and cloisters of the school and set off one solitary mournful bong from Big Brian.

Milk and Spoon thanked the boys one last time and each leaned forward to kiss them on the cheek.

Mildew and Sponge blushed and quivered like strawberry jellies.

'Has the world gone mad?' said Kenningworth. 'Or is that your third kiss of the evening, Mildew?'

Mildew shrugged and smiled dizzily.

'Might we see what you really look like,' asked Sponge, 'as we may never meet again?'

'Yes,' agreed Mildew. 'So that we can recall your true selves when we revisit this scene later in our memories.'

'You may not like what you see,' said Milk.

'You may be repelled,' said Spoon. 'Or even disgusted.'

'Come now,' said Mildew. 'Sponge and I have toughened up a little during the course of this adventure. I'm certain we will be able to take it in our stride.'

'Agreed,' said Sponge.

Milk and Spoon turned to face each other, nodded as if in agreement and then turned back to the boys.

Their disguises disappeared in an instant and their girlish faces were replaced by a baffling and hideous casserole of tentacles and teeth.

'Aaaargh!' screamed Sponge.

'Aaaargh!' agreed Mildew.

The aliens switched back to their earlier guise.

'Better?' they asked.

'Yes,' said Mildew and Sponge very quietly.

'Then I suppose this is farewell for us too, my dear,' said the Headmaster.

'Affirmative,' agreed Miss MT2T.

'Perhaps we may meet again,' said the Headmaster. 'One never knows.'

'Highly … unlikely,' said Miss MT2T. 'Although still … statistically possible.'

Miss MT2T leaned forward with a wheeze and a clank and gave the Headmaster a kiss on his cheek before turning to the girls.

'Intoxicating creature,' said the Headmaster quietly. 'One could travel to the furthest reaches of Lincolnshire and still never find a woman like that, boys.'

'You do realise she is mechanical, sir?' said Mr Luckless, coming to stand beside them.

'Mechanical or not, she's a dashed handsome thing and I shall miss her greatly.'

The Headmaster's lip began to quiver. Mr Luckless sighed and the boys could tell he was thinking about Miss Livia, his Roman romance. Sponge suddenly had the distinct impression that he was being watched and turned round to see a giant floating eyeball hovering behind him.

'Aaaargh!' he screamed.

'Aaaargh!' screamed the others when they turned to see what Sponge was screaming about.

'It's Kevin!' said Mildew. 'We forgot about him … her … whatever …'

'It looks sad,' said Sponge.

It was true. Kevin did look sad.

'This is an Occulox from Brizane 7,' said Milk. 'The Neenor enslave them and force them to spy for them. But they are not by nature bad creatures at all.'

'It's a bit lost, I suppose,' said Mildew. 'Rather far from home.'

'We'll take Kevin with us,' said Milk. 'If you'd like that, Kevin?'

Kevin nodded.

'Brizane 7 is on the way for us,' said Spoon. 'We

can drop her off. We'll also take the Neenor mechanical spiders with us. Best not to leave those lying around. The Neenor vessel becomes unstable when not in contact with their brain waves and should self-destruct harmlessly round about now …'

There was a muffled '*P*hut!' from up on Pug's Peak.

'There will be no trace of its existence except for a rather bad smell for a few days.'

Lamps were lit and the Maudlin Towers boys and staff followed Miss MT2T and the girls up to the top of Pug's Peak and they stood in a wide arc while the aliens waved their final farewells and entered their space-carriage. Their constellation of lamps were mirrored by the stars shining above in the soot-black sky.

After a minute or two the ground began to shake and the craft to glow and hum, making some of the nearby sheep shriek with fear. The glow became brighter and the hum grew louder and louder as the space-carriage broke free from the peat in which it was embedded.

Then there was a great flash of light and slowly the craft rose up from the top of the hill. It seemed not much bigger than the portion they had been able to see, but as it gained height it grew in size, wing-like appendages unfolding like the petals of a huge flower. The mechanical spiders rose slowly from the ground and to gasps from the observers were borne gracefully towards the alien craft, where large doors opened and they disappeared inside.

The craft hovered for a while, slowly revolving, and then blasted up towards the heavens, disappearing in a sparkling plume of twinkling rainbow lights.

And then it was gone, and all was as though it had never been there.

Apart from the massive hole in the ground.

The awestruck crowd stared up at the night sky in silence for a while until they began to fidget and grow restless and a little bored and the Headmaster suggested that perhaps they should all go back inside for a nice cup of tea.

Just as they were turning, Sponge noticed a star moving across the sky, getting larger and larger until it became clear it was heading straight for them.

Before they could even dive for cover, however, there was a flash of light and a booming voice.

'Behold the Great One.'

There, hovering above them was a huge shining image of Mr Stupendo.

'You may have defeated the Neenor,' he boomed. 'But you will never defeat me. I will –'

The image suddenly went *pffft*, shrank to a tiny point of light and then disappeared altogether.

Mildew turned to see Kenningworth pointing the strange object he had brought from the future up at the sky.

'Seems like it wasn't broken, after all,' said Kenningworth.

'Well,' said the Headmaster. 'Following that unpleasantness, shall we now retire to the dank embrace of the school?'

Everyone moved away, discussing the strange events of that day. Mildew patted Kenningworth on the back. Sponge nudged Mr Luckless.

'I wonder if Miss Bronteen might like some company on the walk down,' he said.

'Oh,' replied Mr Luckless. 'Yes. She might. Thoughtful of you, Spongely-Partwork.'

'I meant you, sir,' he replied.

'Oh. Quite. I see.'

Mr Luckless ambled over to where the English teacher stood, staring up into the heavens.

'I always feel so small and insignificant when I look at the night sky,' said Miss Bronteen.

Mr Luckless nodded.

'Although, if we are so small and insignificant, how much smaller must our troubles be,' he said with a smile.

To Mildew and Sponge's astonishment, Miss Bronteen returned his smile.

'Would you care to walk back to the school in a reasonably close yet respectful proximity to one another?' said Mr Luckless.

'Yes,' said Miss Bronteen. 'I'd like that very much.'

Mildew and Sponge smiled as they followed their teachers back to the school.

'That didn't seem quite such an effort,' said Mildew as they walked down. 'You know – climbing up Pug's Peak again.'

'I know what you mean,' said Sponge. 'It felt quite easy this time.'

'Maybe we should climb it more often,' said Mildew. 'To keep our fitness levels up.'

The boys stared at each other for a moment. Then both burst out laughing and continued at a brisk chuckle all the way back to the school.

## Everything is Back to Normal

The following day, the boys insisted that Mildew and Sponge take them to the bothy to see the site of the time machine. They filed in and stared for a long time at the empty patch of floor.

They had insisted on hearing a detailed description of Mildew and Sponge's adventures in time and were all rather jealous – even of the dangerous parts.

'So you're saying it could appear at any moment?' said Kenningworth.

'In theory,' said Mildew. 'Assuming someone took it into the future before we sent it back to the dinosaurs with Mr Stupendo.'

The boys continued to stare at what was in effect, and in reality, just a cobweb-strewn stone wall and filthy tiled floor.

'So *you* might appear?' said Hipflask. 'You might appear now, in front of yourselves?'

'Not us,' said Sponge, rather enjoying this unfamiliar position as expert. 'We'd know if that had happened. We'd remember. Because we'd already have done it.'

'Only if we came from the past, Sponge,' said Mildew. 'Who knows if we get our hands on the time machine again in the future and come back to this actual moment.'

'Of course you would know that you had done that in the past by the time you get to that future point,' said Furthermore, tapping his fingers together. 'While not necessarily knowing now. So in theory you could indeed get access to the time machine and appear now, surprising yourselves entirely.'

'Indeed,' said Mildew, peering at him with a pained expression. 'Well done. You're getting the hang of it.'

The boys looked back towards the space where this hypothetical appearance might take place but the space persisted in being empty.

'Well, this is exciting, I must say,' said Kenningworth.

'Oh, you're just grumpy because you didn't get to use it more,' said Mildew.

Kenningworth smiled. He had to admit it was true.

'Where would you go to, Kenningworth?' said Mildew with a smile. 'If you could have another go?'

'Oh, I don't know,' said Kenningworth. 'I've always had a soft spot for the Egyptians. I wouldn't mind having a look round one of those pyramids.'

'The Crusades for me,' said Enderpenny.

'I'd like to have a long chat with Sir Isaac Newton,' said Furthermore.

'Well, I'd –' began Filbert.

'You can only travel in time, not in space,' said Mildew. 'Sorry – did we not mention that? One can only travel back and forth on the timeline of this particular place.'

'But that's not fair,' said Kenningworth. 'What good is that? I'm immediately less jealous.'

'In any case,' said Mildew, 'something tells me we've seen the last of the time machine.'

Kenningworth sighed. The boys filed out, their heads heavy with disappointment, and Mildew and Sponge stood in the doorway of the bothy watching them trudge towards the ha-ha. Sponge smiled and shook his head.

'These recent perils seem to have brought us all together, Mildew,' said Sponge. 'The boys, the staff, everyone. Some good has come of all this danger.'

'Well said. I believe you're right. Even Kenningworth has shed some of his odiousness. I think things may be a lot more tolerable in the school from now on.'

'Particularly for Mr Luckless and Miss Bronteen,' said Sponge.

'Yes,' said Mildew. 'Who'd have thought it? Good work there, old egg.'

To their amazement there was a flash and a whine behind them in the bothy and they ran back inside to find the time machine returned and seated in it was the very history teacher to whom they had so recently been alluding.

'Mr Luckless!' said Mildew and Sponge.

He looked a little startled to see them and blinked at them through his glasses, taking them off to clean them with his handkerchief.

'Boys!' he said. 'What are you doing here?'

'We could ask the same of you, sir,' said Mildew.

'True,' said Mr Luckless. 'You don't seem very surprised at my appearance.'

'We've seen your black eye before, sir,' said Sponge. 'You've come further into the future than you think.'

'Have I?' said Mr Luckless. 'I must have misread the dials and ended up here instead of my correct time.'

'That's exactly it, sir,' said Sponge.

'Are you sure?' said Mr Luckless.

'Yes, sir. You told us yourself,' said Mildew, remembering the conversation they'd had as they'd climbed Pug's Peak to confront the Neenor.

'Did I?' he said. 'I don't recall.'

'That's because you haven't said it yet, sir,' said Sponge.

Mr Luckless opened his mouth, thought for a while and then closed it again.

'Never mind. What's happening, boys? What excitement am I in for?'

'Well, sir,' said Mildew. 'There has been a spot of bother recently involving alien girls, giant floating eyeballs and huge murderous mechanical spiders …'

'Good Lord,' said Mr Luckless, staring at them. 'That sounds terrifying. I'm rather glad I've missed it.'

'Except that you haven't missed it, sir,' said Sponge. 'You just don't know about it yet.'

Again, Mr Luckless winced as his brain struggled to keep up.

'You're right, of course,' said Mr Luckless. 'Time travel is a mind-slapping business, isn't it?'

'It is, sir,' agreed Mildew.

An awkward silence ensued in which Mr Luckless began to feel a little self-conscious sitting in the time machine and the boys struggled to think of what they could say to their teacher that would not cause further trouble or confuse matters.

'Perhaps it might be best if I just go straight back,' said Mr Luckless. 'I might meet myself and then where would we be? I feel like my journeys in this contraption have not all been best judged.'

'You did meet Miss Livia, sir,' said Mildew. 'So not all bad.'

Mr Luckless smiled.

'Yes,' he said. 'Not all bad. Nothing ventured, eh?'

'And who knows what the future might have in store for you, sir?' said Mildew.

'Did you just wink, Mildew?' said Mr Luckless. 'Why are you smirking?'

'Anyway, sir,' said Sponge. 'I think it might be for the best if you head on back to the past.'

Mr Luckless nodded, still peering at Mildew. He grabbed hold of the lever on the time machine.

'Before I go,' he said, 'might I enquire how everything is at the moment? You mentioned some fairly terrifying predicaments. How fares Maudlin Towers on this particular day?'

Mildew and Sponge smiled.

'Everything is back to normal, sir,' said Mildew.

'Excellent,' said Mr Luckless, and in a flash and with a whine, he was gone.

# Love is a Curious Fish

**M**ildew and Sponge lay on their beds reading books from the library. They had become unaccountably intrigued by books of a more romantic leaning ever since the departure of the alien girls. Mildew put down his copy of *Swoons by Moonlight* by Susanna Smoothly and sighed.

'Love is a curious fish, isn't it, Sponge?' said Mildew.

'I suppose it is, now you come to mention it,' Sponge replied, lowering his book too.

'Although it makes the world go round, they say,' said Mildew. 'Look at old Luckless and Miss Bronteen.'

They gazed off wistfully. Several minutes wafted by.

'I shall miss those girls,' said Mildew. 'Even though they had more tentacles than perhaps they ought.'

'They say love is blind.'

'Not that blind, Sponge,' said Mildew. 'But all the same.'

They returned to their wistfulness for a moment. Mildew licked his lips, clearly struggling to find the right formula of words with which to frame his next question.

'Did you get at all wibblish about Spoon?' he said.

'What?' said Sponge, blushing and spluttering a mite. 'Me? No. Of course not. If anything I thought it was you who – whom – were – was – a bit wibblish about Felicity Fallowfield.'

'Of course not!' said Mildew.

'Milk, then,' said Sponge.

'Milk?' spluttered Mildew. 'Milk? Me? Me and Milk? Of course not. No. No.'

'Or Ella. The girl from the future? She kissed you. More than once.'

'Really, Sponge,' said Mildew with a grin. 'I can't be held responsible for my irresistibility. It is a curse as much as a blessing.'

The boys returned to their books.

'Girls, eh?' said Mildew after a while.

'Indeed,' said Sponge.

'I think this moment calls for a stiff biscuit, Sponge,' said Mildew.

'I think you're right,' said Sponge. 'I'll certainly join you if you're having one.'

Mildew got up and sauntered over to his locker.

'It just so happens that I have a batch of the finest bourbons from Furtnose and Mayfly.'

'Gosh,' cried Sponge, wide-eyed.

'Oh, yes,' said Mildew with a waggle of his eyebrows. 'I've been saving them for just such an occasion.'

Mildew opened the drawer of his bedside locker.

'What on earth?!' he cried. 'There are only two left!'

After staring in confusion for quite a while, he pulled out a piece of paper.

'What is it?' asked Sponge.

'It's a note,' said Mildew, reading it for the seventh time.

'From whom?'

'From Milk.'

'What does it say?'

'It says,'

The boys stared at the note, then at each other, then at the note again.

'I've suddenly lost all interest in girls, Sponge.'

'Me too,' said Sponge.

The two boys walked over to the window and stared up into the sky. It was dusk and stars were beginning to twinkle in the twilight. A full moon was rising above Pig's Pike like a massive dinner plate – but without any dinner on it.

There was a long and wolfish howl from outside.

'Oh no,' said Sponge. 'You don't think Mr Particle may have had another trip in the time machine?'

'I fear that may be the case,' said Mildew.

'What should we do?' said Sponge.

Mildew shrugged.

'Biscuit?' he said with a sigh.

'Why not?' said Sponge.

Maudlin Towers
Near Lower Maud-
lin
Cumberland
England

Dear Parents

Do you remember how I used to complain that Maudlin Towers was ~~mind~~ mind-smotheringly boring? Well never again! The Mildew brain is utterly boggled!! I would actually welcome a week or two of unrelieved tedium and so I'm looking forward to the Christmas hols with even more enthusiasm than usual.

Fondest regards
Arthur Mildew Esq
x x x

PS Please send more biscuits

Maudlin Towers
Near Lower Maudlin
CuMberland
England

Dear Aunt Bernard

Mildew and I have had yet more
adventures. We have them all the
time now. ~~Although~~ It's very
exciting. Although also quite
~~exhay~~ ~~exan~~ tiring. And sometimes
painful! But I have been ~~occaso~~
occasionally Quite brave (for
a Spongely-Partwork).

Sorry to hear you got your
beard caught in the mangle. Again

Your loving nephew
Algernon
xxx xS Please send more
biscuits

Planet Z51a
Near Planet Z51b
Glum Galaxy
Universe

Dear Mildew and Sponge

We hope this letter reaches
you. The Interplanetary postal
system is very ureliable

Thank you again for saving us
(and Earth and possibly the
entire universe!!!) from the
Neenor and sorry for taking
the biscuits

Best wishes
Milk and Spoon
x
PS Please send biscuits

# MAUDLIN TOWERS

## is riddled with mysteries ...

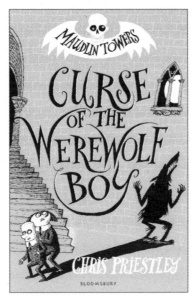

Is that a Viking in the school grounds?

Could there be a ghost in the attic?

Is there a werewolf wandering the corridors?

More importantly, who has stolen the School Spoon?

Can Mildew and Sponge save the day (and Christmas)?

A time-travelling, brain-boggling, mirth-making
adventure awaits!

Turn over now for a sneak peek!

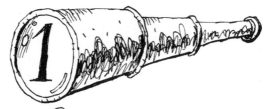

# A Viking in the Ha-ha

Mildew and his friend Sponge were taking a much needed breather on the twice-weekly jog up the side of Pig's Pike. They stood panting, gazing down at the blackened and gloom-laden, gargoyle-infested monstrosity that was their school.

Maudlin Towers School for the Not Particularly Bright Sons of the Not Especially Wealthy sat between the twin hills of Pug's Peak and Pig's Pike in the windswept north country of Cumberland, squatting like an obscenely ornate jet brooch pinned to the bosom of a sour-faced duchess.

Mildew's full name was Arthur Mildew, but no one in the school used first names. Sponge's full name was Algernon Spongely-Partwork, but everyone called him Sponge. They were not happy.

'I'm not happy, Sponge,' said Mildew.

'Me neither,' said Sponge with a sigh.

Mildew helped Sponge take off the backpack that their criminally insane sports teacher, Mr Stupendo, insisted the boys wore on these runs as an extra layer of torture. Mildew groaned with the effort, dropping the backpack to the ground.

'What on earth have you got in there?' he said. 'It weighs a ton.'

'Stupendo caught me filling it with socks again and forced me to load it up with the contents of my trunk.'

Mildew opened the pack and saw items of clothing, shoes, several books and a brass telescope.

'Why on earth do you have a telescope?' he asked.

'I don't really know,' said Sponge. 'My Uncle Tarquin bought it for me last Christmas. I'd forgotten I even had it to be honest. I wish I hadn't.'

'Bad luck,' said Mildew. 'It's rather heavy.'

'I know. By the way – why have you got a bandage on your arm, Mildew?' asked Sponge. 'Did you have an accident in the half-term hols?'

'I've tried to tell you three times now, Sponge,' said Mildew. 'But every time I do, you start to hum to yourself and I get interrupt–'

'Put some pep into it, Mildew!' shouted Mr Stupendo, stroking his horribly large mustachios, his bald head glistening like a damp egg. 'Why, at your age I could lift a dead sheep over my head with barely a bead of sweat!'

Mr Stupendo had been a circus strongman before the life of a sports teacher had tragically caught his eye.

'But, sir,' pleaded Mildew, 'my knees.'

'Nonsense,' said Mr Stupendo, cuffing him round the ear and sending him sprawling headlong into the bracken. 'You're far too young to have knees, Mildew. Come on! The last one to the top is a Russian.'

Mr Stupendo bounded up the path. There were pitiful groans from the boys around him as Mildew got to his feet, and their wretched, downtrodden whining suddenly stirred something in him.

'Look here,' he cried, waving his fist in the air. 'What say we show old Stupido what we're made of and beat the old hippo to the top?'

'Shut up, Mildew, you blister,' said Kenningworth, cuffing him playfully round the ear and sending him sprawling into the bracken once again.

Mildew saw the boys disappearing up the track as he got to his feet. He spat out a piece of the indigenous flora and stared down at Maudlin Towers, a cloud-shadow darkening its already grim and grimy, gargoyle-encrusted walls. *Surely*, he thought, *this must be the very worst of schools.*

'Are you all right?' said Sponge.

'I suppose so,' said Mildew with a sigh that he hoped might hint at the enormity of his despond.

'Someone needs to teach Kenningworth a lesson,' said Sponge. 'My mother says he –'

'Shhh,' said Mildew, pointing down towards the school grounds. 'Never mind Camelfroth or your mother. What's that?'

'What?' said Sponge.

'There!' said Mildew. 'Running along the bottom of the ha-ha.'

'The ha-ha?' said Sponge.

'Yes,' said Mildew. 'The ha-ha.'

'The ha-ha?' said Sponge.

'Stop saying ha-ha!' said Mildew.

'But what do you mean?' said Sponge. 'What are you talking about?'

'The ditch at the end of the sports field, you chump,' said Mildew. 'It's called a ha-ha.'

'Oh,' said Sponge. 'Really? What's it for?'

'To stop sheep wandering into the school grounds,' said Mildew.

'Why on earth would sheep want to wander into the school?' said Sponge, shaking his head and smiling. 'If I were them I'd –'

'Never mind that,' said Mildew. 'Look! There!'

Sponge followed Mildew's pointing finger. Running along the bottom of the ha-ha was a man. That was quite extraordinary in itself as the only man in Maudlin Towers with any inclination to move at speed was high above him leading a chorus of 'Mildew is a Russian!'

But more unusual still was the fact that this man appeared to be wearing a winged helmet and carrying, albeit with some difficulty, what looked, even from that distance, remarkably like a large axe.

'Wait,' said Mildew, and rummaging around in Sponge's backpack, he produced the telescope.

Mildew searched for the figure and focused in on its blurred form.

'There's a Viking in the ha-ha!' said Mildew.

'A Viking? But there can't be,' said Sponge.

'And yet there is,' said Mildew, handing him the telescope.

The boys stared at the Viking in silent amazement as he disappeared out of sight behind a laburnum bush. Before they could say anything, Mildew and Sponge were knocked down like skittles and trampled on by the rest of the boys as they returned from the peak of Pig's Pike.

'Last one to the bottom is a poet!' trumpeted Mr Stupendo as he bounded by.

# A Kerfuffle in the Corridor

ildew and Sponge returned to the school to shower and get changed. If anything, the boys dreaded this more than the exercise itself, the freezing water for the shower coming straight from the beck that ran – rather quicker than the boys – down the side of Pug's Peak.

They dressed as hurriedly as possible and headed off to discuss the mysterious sighting, finding a quiet spot just outside the trophy room.

'Who shall we tell first about the Viking, Mildew?' said Sponge when his jaws had finally stopped rattling with the cold. 'Although I wonder if they'll believe us.'

'Of course they will,' said Mildew. 'Why wouldn't they?'

'Well, I saw it myself and I scarcely believe it,' said Sponge.

'I know what you mean,' said Mildew. 'We need to pick our moment. We don't want to be mocked.'

'Any more than usual,' said Sponge.

'Quite,' said Mildew. 'Oh no, here comes Kenningworth. Quick – in here.'

The boys ducked into the trophy room as Kenningworth and some of the other boys strode down the corridor towards them. They said nothing until they heard the footfalls die away.

The trophy haul at Maudlin Towers was a sorry sight. The school had a long history of failure in almost every branch of the sporting arena. Were it not for the school's own tournaments – like the dreaded Fell-Runner's Cup – the room would be empty save for a couple of items of special significance to the school's history, like the much revered School Spoon.

'Did you hear that?' said Sponge.

'What?'

'It sounded like breathing.'

'Breathing?'

'In the room with us. But not us.'

Mildew and Sponge surveyed the room but saw no sign of anyone else.

'There's no one here, Sponge,' said Mildew. 'You're imagining things.'

Sponge didn't look convinced.

'Can we go, Mildew? I don't like it.'

'Of course,' he said with a smile. 'You are such a –'

Suddenly there was a loud sneeze and both boys almost leaped out of their skin.

'Eeeek!' squeaked Sponge, knocking into Mildew, who banged into one of the cabinets, nearly knocking it over.

They hurried from the room without a backward glance and off to their maths lesson with Mr Painly, who walked to the blackboard and began to write in chalk thereon.

'Very well. If x = 5 and y = Brazil, what is the square root of Thursday?'

# MAUDLIN TOWERS

## is riddled with mysteries ...

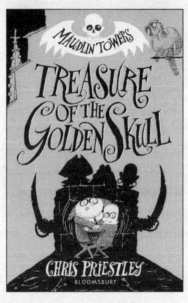

Could there be buried treasure in the school grounds?

Why have all the teachers been replaced by pirates?

What is that no-good nose-hair Kenningworth up to?

And who is that strange new boy called ... um ... Newboy?

Can Mildew and Sponge save the day (and their school)?

A treasure-hunting, extra-thrilling
rib-tickling adventure awaits!

THE AUTHOR

# About the Author

Chris Priestley was born and grew old. He has lived in various places for varying amounts of time. He enjoys eating toast and looking at things. Despite all attempts to stop him, he has written and illustrated this book himself. The relevant authorities have been alerted.

# Do you dare read all the
## *Tales of Terror?*

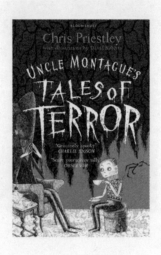

Edgar can't resist the strange and twisted stories
his Uncle Montague tells when he goes to visit
him in his creaky old house. Tales of gruesome
curses and unquiet ghosts trip off his tongue.
He seems to have an endless supply.

But what is Montague's own connection to the
spine-chilling stories he spins? As night draws in,
Edgar begins to suspect that his uncle has saved
the most terrifying twist till last …

'Genuinely spooky' Charlie Higson

'Scare yourselves silly' *Observer*

# Do you dare read all the *Tales of Terror*?

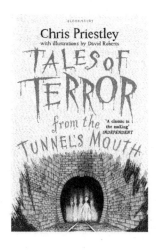

Robert is taking the train by himself for the first time, and he's expecting a thrilling journey. But when the train stalls at the mouth of a gaping tunnel and an elegant woman suggests whiling away the hours with stories, Robert realises he is destined for something much, much spookier …

These are tales with a difference, each one more deliciously chilling than the last. Who is this mysterious storyteller, and why are her tales so dark and bizarre?

'A wonderfully nightmarish journey of the imagination' *Daily Mail*

'A classic in the making' *Independent*

# Do you dare read all the
## *Tales of Terror?*

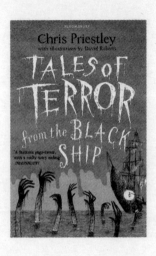

On a storm-lashed night, two sick children wait alone for the doctor. But instead a young sailor knocks on the door, begging for shelter. In return he offers them stories.

Ethan and Cathy love hair-raising tales, and the sailor knows plenty – of plagues and pirates and the terrors of the sea. But it's only as the new day dawns that the children will learn the most blood-curdling tale of all. And that they are at the heart of it …

'Wonderfully macabre and beautifully crafted stories' Chris Riddell

'A fantastic page-turner with a really scary ending' *Independent*